CONTENTS

Prologue

Standing in front of the mirror, the girl who looks back at me is sad, ugly, and just not me. The girl looking at me is Jennifer Hamilton Wade, daughter of Emily Hamilton and Leonard Wade. I was born with a silver spoon in my mouth, just like my parents. They had an arranged marriage, and tonight, we talked about *my* arranged marriage. My parents must think we're back in the twenties or something. There is no way I'm marrying Jonathan Elliott Defoe III. Don't get me wrong, he is good-looking and sexy, but he's too polished for me. I don't want to date him. I don't want to marry him, and I certainly don't want to live with him for the rest of my life.

"Just meet him," my father said.

"He's lovely," my mother said.

"Just accept that you're going to marry him, Jennifer. We have given you everything in this life, so you owe us this," Mother says.

Tonight, he came to dinner. Not a small, intimate, family dinner. No way. That would be too '*normal*'. No, my parents hosted a dinner for all the local aristocracy, no less. At dinner, they proceeded to embarrass both Jonathan and me by telling everyone we're getting married. I didn't even argue with them because there was no point. What they say goes. If I want to live with that silver spoon in my mouth for the rest of my life and have everything I've ever wanted, except love and passion, then I will marry Jonathan.

Little do they know that I have my own plans and they certainly don't include Jonathan, or Mum and Dad, for that matter.

I smile at the reflection in the mirror and slowly take off my pencil skirt and twinset. I leave the pearls that are hanging around my neck like a noose until last. I wipe my 'barely there' make-up off and brush my long black hair. When all traces of Jennifer have gone, I start to get dressed in my mini skirt, which my father would not approve of. Next comes the boob tube which barely covers my ample breasts.

After twirling around in front of the mirror, I start to apply my make-up, which is nothing like the make-up I was wearing earlier. This make up is dark, loud, sparkling, and slutty. I love it.

Next is my necklace, which is a far cry from my pearls. This necklace looks like it's made out of barbed wire. It's not though, and the points don't hurt me. It makes me feel badass, and when I go out prowling, I need to feel badass.

My over the knee boots feel so soft as I pull them up over my smooth, tanned legs. As I zip them up, a frisson of electricity runs through me. I can feel the transformation in my veins. I'm not sure my smile can get any bigger, but I know I have one more change to instigate.

The final piece of the puzzle is my wig. Not just any wig, but a bright pink, short, cropped wig. As soon as it's on my head, it makes me feel different. It makes me feel like my alter ego, Pinkie.

Pinkie is a sassy, sarcastic girl who prowls the streets looking for love. She doesn't want the young, gorgeous, influential men her parents want her to have; she prefers the older, more distinguished men. Call her weird, sick, or whatever words you want. Pinkie doesn't care.

What Pinkie wants, Pinkie fights for.

The Birth of Pinkie

Three Months Ago

I am sick of Mother and Father trying to run my life. This isn't the dark ages anymore. They keep telling me which functions I can go to, who I can talk to, and who I should date. This is so hard to deal with. I have conformed for the last nineteen years of my life and now I'm old enough to make my own decisions. Right?

Who am I kidding? I'm just about to go to another dinner to find an eligible bachelor to marry. When did love and passion not count in a marriage? My parents had an arranged marriage. They keep telling me to look at how happy they are and that it works. I don't tell them I hear them arguing nearly every night when they think I'm asleep, and I have done for most of my life.

Father is having an affair with his secretary—how original.

Mother does a lot of charity work to try and keep her out of the house. They are *not* happily married and they can't convince me otherwise. They are definitely not an advertisement for arranged marriages.

I want fierce and uncontrollable passion, the kind that makes my heart hurt when that special person is not near me. I read a lot of romance books and, yes, I want that guy to come along on his white charger and take me away from all of this and what it represents.

The closer I get to being twenty, and the closer I get to my parents insisting I marry someone of their choosing, the more I want to run away from it all. I lie on top of my bed, wishing my life were different. Yes, I have all the money I will ever need and much, much more. But money isn't everything. I laugh when I think that because, growing up, it was all about how much money I had. What could I get Father to buy for me next? Now, I see that money can't buy love. It can only buy misery.

Tonight, I was introduced to William. He was good-looking, wealthy, but he had the personality of a fish. I think even my parents realised he's not someone we want in our family. So, to piss them off, I cozied up to him and flirted with him all night. My parents were appalled, but he enjoyed it. It was hard to extract myself from him when he was leaving though, as he leant down and whispered in my ear, "I can sneak back in a short while when they've gone to bed, if you like?"

"No, thanks," I said quietly as I shook his hand and walked away, leaving my parents to say goodbye and watch him leave the house.

I can hear them arguing as I lie on my bed. I know Mother will come in to me. I hear her footsteps on the stairs, then the landing.

Three... Two... One...

She knocks on the door. "Can I come in, Jennifer, darling?"

I grunt for her to come in.

"Well, what did you think? I thought he was awfully crass. Did you like him, sweetheart?" She is wary, hoping I don't like him.

"I thought he was rude, ignorant, and someone I definitely don't want to spend the rest of my life with."

Mother smiles and I see her stiff shoulders slump down. She obviously didn't like him either. "Thank God," she mutters. "We will try again, darling. We will find the right fit for our family."

You see, this here is my problem. Even when we're discussing my marriage, it's always about the right fit for the *family*. Not once has she mentioned my happiness in all of this.

I roll over so I can't see her. It's quiet for a few

minutes and then she realises I don't want to talk and she leaves the room with a fleeting, "I love you, Jennifer."

After she's closed the door, I roll back over and look at the ceiling. "Why can't I be normal? Why did I have to be born into this life?"

I thump my hands up and down on the soft bed beneath me. I growl as I get more and more frustrated.

"I want to be someone different. I don't want to be Jennifer Hamilton Wade anymore. I want to be able to do the things that I want to do. When I want to do them."

My brain is working overtime, the cogs turning, and I can feel the start of a plan come together. I smile as I climb under the covers, fully dressed, and dream about my immediate future and how I'm going to change things.

After breakfast the next morning, I say to Mother, "I'm going to Harrods today. Do you want anything?"

"Oh, lovely. Are you going for something in particular?"

"No. I'm going to meet Cassandra for lunch."

"Very good. Can you stop in the food hall and get

me some of their Beluga Caviar? We seem to have run out and we might need some soon."

"Of course," I say, standing up and walking around the table to where she's sitting. "Anything for you." I lean down and kiss her on the cheek before leaving the room and heading for my bedroom.

I dress in my most conservative clothes as I always do; beige tailored trousers with a white Ralph Lauren blouse and a camel coloured jumper hanging around my neck. When I look in the mirror, I smile to myself, knowing that, today, everything changes. Today, my alter ego is being born and I intend to embrace it.

Our driver, Tony, is waiting for me at the front of the house. He opens the door for me and waits until I'm fully seated before closing the door. As he sits in the front, he asks, "Where to, Miss Jennifer?"

"Tony, I told you to just call me Jennifer, not Miss Jennifer. Can you take me to Harrods, and then I'll call you when I need collecting? I'm going to browse for a while."

"Certainly, Miss... sorry, Jennifer."

I smile and sit back, thinking of what I intend to buy today.

After a liquid lunch with Cassandra, I catch the Tube over to Earl's Court, as I've heard there are some perfect shops for what I need.

I don't go on the Tube very often, so it's exciting

and exhilarating. The smells and sounds are so alien to me, but I love it. Walking into the first shop I find, Miss Euro, I'm enthralled with what I see. It's beyond my wildest dreams.

Miss Euro is a sex shop. They have everything you can think of and a lot of things that you can't. I walk around with my mouth open, and when I walk to the back of the shop, I see something that's perfect.

High on the wall full of wigs is a bright pink cropped wig.

"Excuse me," I say to the shop assistant. He looks at me and walks towards me.

"Can you get me the pink wig, please?"

He looks me over in my conservative clothes and smiles. "Certainly, Miss." After using a long handle to hook the wig down, he hands it to me. "Do you want me to help you put it on properly?"

I smile. "I would love that, if you don't mind."

He walks towards some seats and mirrors which have light bulbs around them. "Come over and take a seat and I'll show you how to do it correctly."

I take a seat and he brushes out my long black hair. He neatly ties it back and secures it with a hair net. He then puts the wig onto my forehead first and then slowly eases it down over my head, much the same was as I would put on a swimming cap, if I ventured into the swimming pool.

I can see the transformation already. I smile so wide I think my make-up is going to crack. When he has it fully on my head, he looks at me and says, "Hang on there a minute. I'm going to style it properly for you." He rushes off, and when he comes back, he has some scissors and spray in his hands.

It's like watching a master artist at work. He snips here, combs there, sprays everywhere until it looks like a gorgeous style made just for me. When he stands back and says, "Ta da!" I almost start to cry.

He twirls me around in the chair and hands me a mirror so I can see the back of my head. It's gorgeous. Really something else.

"I love it! I want it!"

"Are you going to keep it on?"

"Oh, God, no! My mother would hate this. This is just for special occasions. I want to buy some clothes though. Can you help me out, please?"

"Of course. What kind of clothes do you need?"

"I want to stand out. When I walk into a room, I want everyone to look at me and feel jealous. I want them to hold onto their boyfriends because they will be worried that I'll take them away. Can you make me look like that?"

He nods, and with a flourish, he helps me out of the chair.

After another hour in the shop, I have everything I

need to make the changes I want. Scottie, that's the guy who has been helping me all afternoon, has everything hanging up in the changing room and he's ready for me to make my changes. Then he's going to show me how to apply the make-up I need for the final piece of the puzzle.

I'm so excited, I rush to put the clothes on, and when I put the over the knee boots on, I feel perfect.

I step outside and look in the mirror, clapping my hands. "It's perfect, Scottie. Thank you so much."

"Oh my God, Jennifer. You look amazing."

"No." I shake my head, "Jennifer won't do. I need a new name." I look in the mirror and smile. I turn to face Scottie, and I shake his hand. "Hi, Scottie. I'm Pinkie."

He pulls me into a hug and laughs. "Pinkie, I love it."

After another hour, he has shown me how to do my new make-up. It's very exaggerated and different to the plain, boring colours I use every day. That's what I want though. I want to be different. I want Pinkie to be the complete opposite of Jennifer Hamilton Wade. She stands for everything I want to be, but can't.

"Babe, why don't you come out with me tonight and meet some of my friends? I think they are going to love you," Scottie says.

"I would love that, but I won't be able to come out

until later. I don't want anyone to know Jennifer. I want them to know me as Pinkie. Is that okay?"

"Perfect, darling." He kisses me on the cheek. "Now, we better put all of this away and let you pay for it and get home."

Sadly, I go into the changing room and change back to boring Jennifer. I feel even more boring now I've had a taste of Pinkie. Tony collects me at Earl's Court by the exhibition centre. He doesn't ask any questions, even when he sees all my bags. We drive home in silence.

On The Prowl

Mother has another *eligible bachelor* over for dinner. I'm sick and tired of different men coming over every night, but especially tonight, because I want to go out and meet Scottie. He makes me laugh and he takes me for who I really am, not who everyone thinks I should be.

Tonight's man is Jonathan Elliott Defoe III. His family own a large chain of hotels. Don't get me wrong, he's a nice guy, but he has no interest in me at all. He has clearly been made to come along as his parents sit and talk to my parents. We make small talk, but neither one of us is interested.

Dinner drags by and I keep looking at my rose gold Rolex which Father bought me for my nineteenth birthday a few months ago.

"Do you have somewhere you need to be,

Jennifer?" Jonathan asks, looking at his watch.

I look at him sadly. "Anywhere other than here, to be honest."

He laughs. "Yes, I feel like that too. Any chance we can skip off somewhere together?" I hope he isn't asking me to spend the rest of the evening with him. "As friends, of course," he says, before my mind spirals out of control.

"I have other plans, but thank you for offering to help me out. I can't wait for dinner to be over so I can go to my room and then do a disappearing act and get out of here."

He laughs again and then clears his throat. "Mother, Father, Mr and Mrs Hamilton Wade, it has been a pleasure this evening, but I'm feeling unwell and I need to go home." He winks at me and I rest my hand on top of his and squeeze it slightly.

"Oh my gosh. Jonathan, you didn't say you weren't feeling well," his mother says.

"I wanted to meet Jennifer. And as beautiful as she is, I just don't feel well and need to go home." He stands and covers his mouth then starts to run from the room.

I stand and shout after him, "First door on the left," and follow him out. He pulls me into the downstairs cloakroom with him and we both start laughing, but we have to be quiet.

"Do you think they bought it?" he asks.

"Definitely, especially seeing as you ran out of the room. That was so funny."

We wait for about five minutes and then we come out of the cloakroom and go back into the dining room. Thankfully, they have finished dinner and are drinking coffee.

"Jonathan, darling. We're ready to leave whenever you are," his mother says to him as she feels his forehead.

"I think... I think I need to go and lie down."

His mother takes that as her cue to leave and rustles his father up so that, within ten minutes, the three of them have left and it's just Mother, Father and I.

"I think I'll go to bed too. Jonathan was very nice, Mother. It's a shame he was ill and had to leave early."

"I know, Jennifer. We will find you someone, you know? It's just about getting the right fit."

I can't help but mutter under my breath, "The right fit for who? Goodnight. See you in the morning." I almost run up the stairs. I know she's going to come in and say goodnight to me, so I climb under the covers and turn the light off.

Sure enough, she comes in about twenty minutes later and says she's just checking on me and she will see me in the morning. I wait for another ten minutes before I slowly and quietly get out of bed and start getting ready. My heart is beating fast. Off come the dowdy colours and on go the bright, eclectic colours. The last thing I do is put the wig on, just like Scottie showed me. I look into my floor to ceiling mirror and admire my handiwork. I love it!

Creeping out of my room, I make sure there's no one around and then slip out of the door. A taxi is already waiting for me at the gate to our estate. When I get there, I jump in and tell him to take me to Miss Q's in Earls Court. I tap my foot. My hands are a little sweaty, and I don't know what is going to happen tonight and my adrenaline is at an all-time high. The anticipation of introducing Pinkie to a group of people I've never met before is making my heart beat erratically. Will they like me? I hope they do, I want some friends who know me as I want to be, not who I am.

When the cab drops me off outside, I quickly pay the driver then stand looking at the entrance to Miss Q's. I ring Scottie to let him know I'm outside. I'm not sure I'm brave enough to walk into a pub on my own. That just isn't heard of in my circle of friends.

I look at the red and white striped canopy hanging over the front door, and when I see Scottie making his way outside, I'm relieved.

"Hey, Pinkie," he says, winking at me. "Come and

meet my friends. They're going to love you." He kisses me on both cheeks and takes my hand. He pulls me inside and we go down the stairs into a room which has three pool tables in it, a section where I can see people dancing, and another section where there are people just talking.

He introduces me to his small group of friends. "This is Pinkie, everyone. I met her today and I just know she is going to be so much fun."

I try to remember everyone's name as I head to the bar to get myself a drink. Scottie comes with me. "Scottie, I've never ordered a drink in a bar before. What do you recommend?"

"Have you never been to a bar before? That is fucking adorable." He laughs. "I think you need to have a Cosmopolitan. It's very posh, just like you."

"Okay, whatever you say. What are you going to have?"

"I'll have the same!" He orders for both of us.

I hit it off with Scottie and his friends who are all so much fun. They have welcomed me with open arms and I can't believe they have been so friendly. My family friends are always so cold with strangers, so this is very new to me. There's Ryan, who's Scottie's boyfriend, Tiffany, who's a blonde bombshell, Jose, who is so gorgeous it hurts to look at him, and then there's Ruby, who has bright red hair.

I'm having so much fun, and after a couple of hours, I'm relaxed and dancing with Tiffany and Ruby when I spot a guy watching me intently.

Ruby sees where I'm looking and nudges my arm. "I think granddad over there is eyeing you up." She laughs.

He has to be over fifty, but, he's quite sexy in an old man kind of way. He keeps looking at me and smiling.

I have more Cosmopolitans. I smile at him. He winks at me. I'm feeling brave. I need to remember I'm Pinkie tonight, not Jennifer.

I walk over to him. "Do I know you?"

He chuckles. "No, but you will soon."

I cringe at his line. "You think?"

He reaches out, puts his hand on my waist, and pulls me in closer to him. He puts his lips to my ear and whispers, "I know so." He then very gently places his lips just under my ear on the soft spot... you know, that spot that sends a message directly to your vagina.

I melt into his touch and moan. What the heck is wrong with me? I usually make men work for a piece of me, but this guy has me wet from a slight touch and a few words.

He lets his grip on my waist loosen slightly and then he smiles his devilishly handsome smile. He has extremely white, straight teeth. He is very well-styled in designer brands.

I step back slightly and look at him closely. He's tanned, and even though he's older than me, he looks like a bit of a cheeky chappie. I could do worse.

"So what about it? Do you fancy going somewhere a bit quieter so I can get to know you better?"

I stifle a laugh. Is this really his chat up line?

"I don't even know your name." I lean in closer to his ear and whisper, "I need to know what name to scream when you make me come."

He takes a deep breath and I know he's trying to think of a comeback. Eventually, he says, "I'm Drew."

"I'm Pinkie," I say, smiling at him. "Take me back to your place and make me scream."

He gives me a wide smile then stands and takes my hand. He pulls me through the pub, and as I go past my friends, he stops and says, "She won't be back later."

Tiffany and Ruby laugh, but Scottie steps forward and puts his hand on Drew's chest. "Wait a minute. We don't know who you are. Pinkie, text me wherever you go and if I don't hear from you within half an hour, I'm going to track your phone. Right?"

"I'll be fine, but yeah, okay." I've never had someone fight for me. I lean forward and kiss him on the cheek. Drew blushes. "Come on then, big guy. Let's move on to the next place."

He smiles at me and continues on his way out of Miss Q's.

He holds his hand out for a black cab and one pulls up straight away. He opens the door for me to get in, and when I do, he follows me in. "The Kensington, please."

I've been to The Kensington a few times. It's a lovely hotel. The rooms aren't cheap; Drew must have money, or he's here on business. I turn to ask him, but he doesn't give me a moment. He leans forward and runs his hand over my cheek and then he pulls me to him and kisses me.

I hesitate, but then his kiss sets off some feelings in between my legs that I haven't had before. Hopefully, his age and experience are just what I need tonight. Most of the men I've messed around with are just after a fumble and are not interested in making me happy. They just want their own release.

I moan; Drew's kisses are hot. I lean into him more and then I startle myself by climbing onto his lap and straddling him. There's not a huge amount of room, but he doesn't care. He puts his hands behind me, on my arse, and he pulls me closer to him. I can feel his rock hard cock. It feels huge.

He pulls back and looks at me, rests his forehead on mine, and says, "This is a surprise. I didn't realise I was going to bring a sexy young lady home with me tonight. I only went out for a quick drink."

He leans forward again and kisses me, pulling me

close again as he starts to push his cock into me. I grind down onto his cock and he starts to moan.

The taxi driver says, "We're here. Thank God for that. I was going to have to pull over and watch in a minute." He laughs.

I know I should be embarrassed, but tonight, I'm Pinkie, and I'm not embarrassed. Climbing off Drew's lap, I sit back in the chair. He pays for the taxi then gets out first. He grabs my hand and pulls me into the hotel before I can change my mind.

Once we're in the lift, he pushes me up against the wall and kisses me again. This time, his hands are roaming over my body. His hand goes to my skirt and I feel it creep underneath, getting closer to my fully waxed lips.

He pulls back slightly. "You're bare. Oh, I'm so lucky." He continues to kiss me and then the lift stops and the doors open. He grabs my hand and pulls me again, this time to his room. As soon as the door is open, he closes it and locks it. Then he takes his jacket off, all the time watching me, watching to see if I run away. I don't. The pink wig has given me a confidence I never knew I had. I drop my jacket to the floor then lift my top over my head and it joins my jacket. He takes his shirt off and then undoes his trousers. All the time we're undressing, we're watching each other intently.

My skirt goes next, then his shoes and socks, his

trousers, and then we're both in our underwear. Me in my bright pink pants and bra and him in his boxer briefs.

He smiles and then helps me out of my bra and pants, but he leaves my boots on; that's fine with me. I take his boxer briefs down and his cock springs to attention. I was right; it is huge.

Taking it in my hand, I slowly lower myself to the floor where I kneel and start pumping my hand up and down his shaft. I can smell his excitement. I stick out my tongue and lick the pre-cum off the end of his cock. All the time I'm watching him, waiting to see what he does.

I lick his cock like an ice-cream and then take him into my mouth. He is huge and I can't take all of it so I use one of my hands to hold the base. When he hits the back of my throat, I moan as the feeling of being full turns me on even more. He fucks my mouth, making me gag, and I have to pull free to get air into my lungs before taking him back in.

After only a few minutes, he pulls away and grabs my arms to pull me up. "That's enough. I won't make it inside you if you carry on. I really want to sink into your hot, sweet pussy."

"Stop talking and get on with-"

He has his hand behind my neck and pulls me

closer. Before I have chance to finish my sentence, his hot tongue is in my mouth, silencing me.

Drew walks me backwards towards the bed, and all of a sudden, he turns me around and pushes me down. My legs are still hanging over the edge of the bed, my feet firmly planted on the floor. I can feel the breeze around my pussy as he grabs a condom and rolls it down his hard shaft.

"I have been looking forward to this moment all night." Drew pushes his cock into my pussy with such a huge thrust that I nearly fall forward, but I catch myself just in time.

Pushing back, I feel him bottom out. When he pulls back out to thrust in again, I meet him thrust for thrust until I cry his name out in release.

He rams me through my orgasm, and then he comes close, he pulls out. Immediately, I turn and take the condom off before taking him in my mouth and swallowing his orgasm as he calls out my name.

When he has finished spurting his cum down my throat, he stops thrusting. I gently run my hand up and down his still hard cock and lick the cum off the end.

"Wow, I don't know what to say about that. We just fucked like animals," Drew says as he sits on the end of the bed.

"I know. Can we do it again?" I ask as I straddle him and assault his mouth with mine.

The Name of the Game

It's been three months since I invented Pinkie, and to say I've had fun is an understatement. Scottie has turned into a really good friend, and so has Ruby. I have slept with lots of men, always older. The guy from my first dalliance has been texting me and we meet regularly for mind-blowing sex. His name is Drew and he runs his own PR company. He lives and works in the States, but he comes over to London every month for a long weekend to meet his English customers. I make sure I'm around to see him when he comes over; he certainly looks after me.

Tonight, Mother has another bachelor coming over for dinner with his parents. She hasn't given up, but I think she understands that I'm not interested in anyone she has to offer me. I keep telling her that I want passion and lust in my relationship, and I don't want to be paired with someone as part of a business deal. She may understand that, but she doesn't believe in it.

"Come along, Jennifer. Hurry up. Thomas will be here shortly with Eva and Derek. We want you to be downstairs waiting for them to get here, not walking down the stairs at the last minute," Mother shouts up the stairs, for the third time in the last half an hour.

I'm really tempted to come downstairs as Pinkie. I laugh, thinking how that would play out. I look in the mirror and all I see is dowdy. I decide to put a little bit of Pinkie into my outfit and put on a black pencil skirt with a black blouse. I have a bright pink camisole underneath which shows across my breasts. I smile. Yes, enough just to tease.

I know I can tease. All the men I sleep with tell me that I'm a big cock tease. I draw them in with my sexy dancing and my obvious love of sex. I like the more experienced man who knows what they're doing and what a woman wants. That doesn't always happen though, and I have been known to walk out during sex when the man is being selfish and not worrying about my needs. I get to the point when they're going to come and then I stop, get up, grab my clothes, put them on as I walk to the door, and then leave. No one is going to just take from my body. They need to give too.

After I walk downstairs, I just get a glimpse of my parents when there's a knock at the front door. I smile at the shock on Mother's face when she sees the little bit of lace showing under my blouse. I open the door and welcome the threesome into the house.

"Hi, I'm Jennifer. You must be Eva and Derek, and this handsome man must be Thomas." I shake hands with them all.

Thomas comes from behind his parents and he takes my breath away. He is gorgeous; the best one yet. I blush when he takes my hand and raises it to his lips. "It's my pleasure, Jennifer," he says.

"Come on in," Mother says, closing the door behind Thomas. I can't take my eyes off him and he won't let go of my hand. I pull it out of his grasp and he follows me into the dining room. He is seated next to me at the table and he pulls out my chair for me to sit down. A gentleman too. Nice.

During dinner, I find out he's training to be a doctor and I know that, if there was something wrong with me, I would want him to look after me. He has a great bedside manner and is a very nice guy. I like him, but I don't want to marry him. His initial handsomeness is a joy, but beyond his looks, he doesn't have a great personality. He is *nice*. I don't want just nice. I don't mind meeting him again, but nothing much will come of it. I think he feels the same as he leans over and says, "I've enjoyed tonight. If you want to get together some time to get the parents off our backs then just let me know."

"Thanks. I might take you up on that one night." I smile at him and he leans over and kisses me on the cheek. I think it's more for our parents' sake than mine.

My phone beeps with a text and I read it. It's from Drew.

How is my sex machine?

I blush, even though I know no one else can see the text.

I'm drying up. When are you coming over to see me?

Ha ha, well I just landed and I'm on my way over to the hotel now. I know it's short notice, but one of my clients wants to see me about expanding their business and it can't wait.

I'm having dinner with my parents right now. Do you want to catch up later?

Hell yeah sugar, I am not waiting another 24 hours till I am inside your sweet, hot body xx

I try not to laugh out loud. I really like him and it suits me that he doesn't live here. I don't want a relationship with him, but his familiarity is comfortable. I enjoy our trysts when he visits. That's enough for me.

Do you think you can handle me? It's been a few weeks you know.

Sugar, I've been thinking of nothing else and my cock is hard just thinking of how hot you are and how wet I make you.

"You're blushing. It must be someone special to make

those cheeks turn that colour," Thomas says, startling me.

"Oh my God. I'm so embarrassed. It's a friend of mine and they are being..." I cough. "...slightly inappropriate." I stifle a laugh.

He doesn't stifle his. "Inappropriate. Well, I can imagine what he said just by looking at your cheeks and your eyes. I would love to be the one to put that look on someone."

"Oh, no. We are just friends. He doesn't get into the country often. My parents don't know though, so I would appreciate if you didn't mention anything."

"Of course not. Maybe we can hang out sometime. I might have misjudged you."

"I'd love that. And Thomas, you have definitely misjudged me."

When they leave, I swap numbers with Thomas. I think he would like Pinkie better than Jennifer, but he won't get to see her. She is my guilty pleasure.

"I'm tired, Mother. I'm going to bed. Thomas was lovely." I kiss Mother and Father on the cheek and start to walk up the stairs.

"I saw you swap numbers." She sounds like she's getting her hopes up.

"We did, but I don't think anything will come of it. I liked him though." My father puts his arm around Mother and pulls her close. I never see any closeness between them and it throws me off for a moment. "I love you both," I say, walking up the stairs to bed.

After I hear them go to bed, I start to get ready to go back out. I hate lying to them, but I love being Pinkie. I love what she represents. It takes me half an hour to get changed and put on my make-up and wig and then I creep back down the stairs and out of the door. I move really quickly down the drive to the waiting taxi.

"The Kensington Hotel, please," I say, and sit back and think about Drew. He's a decent guy. He is always good to me, and I look forward to him visiting London. I know he's fifty, but he doesn't look it and he certainly doesn't act it. He's more virile than any of the guys I've been out with. I don't think he realises how old I am though. It's never cropped up. Neither of us is in this relationship for anything other than fantastic sex.

I send him a quick text so he knows I'm on the way.

I'll be there in twenty minutes. Are you ready for me?

Ready as I will ever be sugar. I need you, I am going to take you, and then we are going out!

Out??

Yeah, my client owns a club and we are going over there to see what it is all about and then talk business.

I'll be in the way Drew. Just fuck me and go without me.

No way sugar. I want you to come with me. I think you'll like it there. I might be able to swing you a job there.

A job? I don't need a job.

You might change your mind when you see what it is. Trust me!

OK, I trust you, but you better be waiting with your cock in your hand, cos I need me some of your big cock!

I get a message with a picture. Drew's cock! I laugh so hard; he really does have a large cock. I save the picture to add to my very own 'wank bank'.

The taxi pulls up outside the hotel. I pay and then make my way inside. The staff smile at me as they have seen me here a few times. The thought crosses my mind that they might think I'm a prostitute, but I don't care.

When I get out of the lift, I make my way down to Drew's room and knock loudly on the door. It doesn't take him long to answer and he is ready for me, his cock is in his hand, and he pushes me up against the door, locks it, and then he puts his hand under my dress to find I'm naked underneath.

"You're ready for me, sugar. You're bare and wet, just how I like your cunt."

He kisses me with the fierce passion of a man taking his last breath of air. While his tongue is fighting with mine, he pushes his cock inside me.

"Oh my God, Drew," I say into his mouth.

"I know, baby. It feels really good." He fucks me hard. I love it. We both topple over the top at the same time.

I lay my head on his shoulder while he holds me up against the door. "Thank God you don't come to visit more often. I'd be raw."

He laughs. "Most women would love for me to visit more often, but not you. Should I be offended?"

"No way! You know this is not a relationship, don't you?"

"Hell yeah, I just thought you might have changed your mind. You're not needy like most women and it throws me off a little. I'm waiting for the bomb to be dropped."

"No bombs from me. I like your cock and your cock likes my cunt. I don't see the problem with that."

He laughs as he pulls out and takes the condom off. As he goes into the bathroom to clean up I take my knickers out of my handbag and put them on. I might be easy, but I'm not that bad.

When he comes out, I'm waiting for him on the chaise longue. He stops and looks at me. "You really are beautiful. Why do you feel that you have to try and be someone else? I know you're hiding something."

"Who says I'm trying to be someone else when I'm with you? What about if I'm trying to be someone else when I'm not with you and this is the person I want to be?"

He helps me off the chair. "I like this version of you, so I'm not complaining. I just want you to be happy."

"I am very happy and, right now, I am extremely happy because that was one amazing orgasm you just gave me." I lean into him and kiss him on the cheek.

He laughs. "Damn right it was. Let's go. I think you're going to enjoy tonight."

There is a taxi waiting for us when we leave the hotel, and after holding the door for me, Drew climbs in after me. He says, "Whiskey Sour, please," and then takes my hand.

"Ooh, I've never been there but I've heard so much about it. It's the talk of the town."

"I know, and Whiskey is my client. Well, Sawyer, her husband, is my client, but they come as a partnership and the club is in her name."

"What do they need you to do for them?"

"They want to open another couple of clubs and they need some PR advice."

"That sounds like fun."

"Their clubs are always fun. Sit back, relax, and enjoy the ride, sugar."

When we arrive outside, the first thing that hits me is that it doesn't look like a club from the outside. Drew pulls me inside and I get a fright because, standing in front of us, is a really big man. He is tall, wide, and he looks scary.

He looks like he's going to stop us going in, then when he sees Drew, he cracks a smile. He is gorgeous.

"Drew, man, How are you? Sawyer said you were coming, but I didn't know you were coming tonight. I thought you would be over tomorrow during the day."

They shake hands and clap each other on the back. "Couldn't wait to get over here, Stig. This is one of my special places."

"Come on in, get yourself a drink, and wait at the bar. I'll let them know you're here."

He looks at me and then back to Drew. "Who is this beauty and when did you have time to meet her?"

"This is Pinkie and I've known her a while now. We hook up whenever I'm over." He pulls me in close to him and kisses me on the cheek.

I hold my hand out to shake his. "Hi. I'm excited about coming here tonight. Drew has been telling me all about it."

He looks me up and down and then shakes my hand. "I'm Stig. Pleased to meet you. Hope you enjoy the show." He reaches out and opens the door into the club. It's funny how you can't hear the music, but when he opens the door, the music is loud. That is some soundproofing. I could do with that in my room at home.

Drew pulls me along to the bar and finds a seat for me. He then leans over the bar and orders me a drink.

"Hey, Spence. How's it going, mate? Can I order a couple of drinks, please?"

"Hey, Drew. Good to see you. What's your pleasure tonight?" the attractive barman asks.

Drew looks at me and smiles. "I'll have a Scotch on the rocks and my lovely lady will have a Cosmopolitan, please."

Spence nods and moves away to make the drinks.

Drew leans into me and says, "I know you're going to enjoy the show tonight and I will reap the rewards later."

I laugh. Just as I'm about to reply, Spence brings back the drinks and the lights go down. I hear Drew say, "Can you tell Whiskey and Sawyer that I'm here and can meet with them when it suits them."

I don't hear Spence's reply. I take a sip of my drink and watch in awe what's happening on the stage. "That's Snow, Spence's girl," Drew says in my ear.

I hear some ballet music and then I see the most beautiful ballet dancer in the history of ballet dancing. She has to be over six foot. She has milk chocolate-coloured skin and she is amazing. The music is haunting and beautiful, kind of hypnotic, then it starts hitting out a club beat and her style of dance changes. Along the way, she has lost her skirt and now her top, but she still has a basque on. She collapses on the ground when the music stops. Everyone in the place stands up and claps their hands.

"Drew, that was amazing. She is so talented." I'm transfixed when she leaves and another woman appears on the stage. She does a jazz number, and then another woman dances in army camouflage.

By the time the lights come back on, I have had three Cosmopolitans and I can't stop staring. There is music being played and some of the audience have started to dance on the dance floor close to the stage. I want to go and join them. I want to try and do what the women did on stage.

Drew is behind me and his hand squeezes my waist. "Are you glad you came this evening?"

"Absolutely. This is so surreal. I never knew this was what Whiskey Sour is. I don't know why I haven't been here before."

"You need to be a member to get in and it takes a lot to be a member."

"I want to come here again, Drew. Can you get me a membership?" I turn around and kiss him, sucking his tongue into my mouth.

He chuckles into my mouth. "I'll see what I can do, sugar."

Spence interrupts us with a cough. "Sawyer and Whiskey asked if you can stick around after closing to see them."

"Yes, of course. That is not a problem. Is that okay with you, Pinkie? Or do you want to go home?"

"No fucking way! I want to meet everyone. This place is fantastic."

He chuckles again.

The second half of the show is as good as the first. The girls do something they call freestyle. The DJ plays a random piece of music and they have to dance to it in their own distinctive style. The girls all dance on the stage together and it's something else to see the different types of dance to the same piece of music.

If I thought that was good, then the finale just blows me away. I am hooked. I love this place. I want to get up on that stage and dance with them.

When the lights come back on, I'm still thinking about the girls dancing on the stage. Some of the audience is dancing and I want to join them.

Drew obviously sees that I want to dance and he says, "Go dance, sugar. I know you want to."

I don't say anything, but get off the chair and walk towards the dance floor. I move to the music and I don't hear anything going on around me, just the music in my ears. I close my eyes and lose myself in the rhythm.

The song changes and my moves change with it. I feel like I'm in another world. I look over to Drew to see him watching me and he smiles at me and then turns and kisses a woman on the cheek and shakes the hand of the gentleman next to her. They must be Whiskey and Sawyer; I'll leave him to talk business for a while.

I ask someone where the toilets are and make my way down the corridor towards them. The walls are red velvet and they have a sign that says, 'The Sweet Girls of Whiskey Sour, where the girls are sweet, but their dancing is not!' Then there are pictures of the girls on the walls with their names underneath them.

Snow is the girl who was doing ballet, Dee Dee did the jazz number, and Sage was dancing in the army camouflage. I look at the pictures for a few minutes before I realise I'm not alone in the corridor. I can feel someone's eyes roaming over my body.

I turn slowly, but I don't see anyone. I hear someone though. "Did you enjoy the show?" a deep voice says, vibrating through my body.

I still can't see anyone. "I did. Where are you?"

"I'm here," he says. I still can't see him.

"Oh, you're so funny." I move towards the toilets, and as I reach out to open the door, my body is slammed up against the wall.

"Don't laugh at me. I saw you at the bar with Drew. Is he man enough for you? You look like you need a real man to take care of you."

"He's more man than you would ever be."

"How do you know that?"

"His cock strains to get out of his trousers when he gets this close to me." I lean my arse back to try and feel him. "Unlike you!"

He laughs, pushing into me and I feel his cock against me. He grinds it into the cheeks of my arse. "Do you feel that? Now that's a cock."

He's right; he is huge, even bigger than Drew. I want it and I haven't even seen the owner. I reach my hand back and grab it. This might be the only time I get to touch it. I squeeze it hard and he gasps.

"That's only a cocktail sausage. I prefer foot longs. Now, if you can move that..." I squeeze it again, because I don't really want to let go yet. "... then I can go to the bathroom like I intended before you accosted me."

He leans into me and sucks my earlobe. God, this man's body is setting mine on fire and I don't even know who he is or what he looks like. At this moment in time, my body doesn't care.

"Do you want me to give you a hand? Or better yet, you could give me a hand instead."

"I'm good at using my own hand, thank you." I push back, trying to get him away from me. "Now, can you please let me go?"

"I'll move this time, but I know that you'll be thinking about me later when Drew pushes his wrinkly, old cock inside you."

I laugh. "Drew's is so big, it doesn't have wrinkles." For some reason, I find this hilarious and can't stop laughing.

He starts to laugh too. "I was just clutching at straws anyway." He reaches out and covers my eyes with his hand and turns my head over my shoulder. Then he kisses me. I want to fight back. I want to bite his tongue, but for some reason, I can't. His mouth is like a drug. I want more of it.

I'm wet from his kiss; I want to ravage him. I moan. He moans. He pulls away and lets me go before I can take a breath, and when I turn around, he's gone. My heart is going mad. My breath is laboured and I daren't turn around. I lean my head against the wall and take a deep breath. What the fuck just happened?

After I've been to the toilet, I go back out to find Drew still talking business with Whiskey and Sawyer. I do what my body wants me to do: dance. I swear the music is speaking to me. The words of all the songs are mirroring how I feel right now. How I feel after being accosted in the corridor. I feel sexy, dirty, and fucking horny.

I laugh at the next song; it's Jermaine Stewart's *We Don't Have To Take Our Clothes Off*.

Listening to the lyrics, I move my body to the words, thinking about the mystery man in the corridor. I laugh, thinking about what he said about Drew's wrinkly cock.

I realise I'm swaying to the music and running my hands over my body. I need Drew to satisfy me. He's still talking business. Fuck.

When I look over to him, I see that they're all watching me dance. I got so carried away with the feeling of the music running through my veins that I forgot I wasn't alone. I blush and stop swaying my body then walk back over to them at the bar.

Drew pulls me in and whispers in my ear. "Don't expect me to move right now. I am as hard as the rock of Gibraltar. That was fucking hot, sugar."

I giggle and take a sneak peek down at the bulge in his trousers. I whisper back, "I can take care of that if you need me to."

He laughs, grabs my hand and then introduces me to Whiskey and Sawyer.

"Hi. This is one amazing club you guys have here," I say, extending my hand. "I can't believe I haven't been here before."

"Thanks," Whiskey says, smiling. "You can move, girl! I bet every man in here is tenting right now." She laughs and looks around her.

A lot of the guys are looking at me, but I just assumed that was because of my pink hair; it makes me stand out. I laugh back at her. "Oops!"

Sawyer looks at me and says, "This is not an oops moment. What you just did out there on the dance floor is fucking sexy as hell." Whiskey turns around to look at him, pretending to be angry. "Baby, no one is as sexy as you and I don't have a tent like Drew."

I blush and Drew says, "Fuck off, Sawyer," as we all look at his trousers.

Whiskey laughs. "What you just did is what we aim to do with every dance on that stage."

I blush. I know Drew tells me I'm sexy, but he just wants to bury his cock balls deep inside me, so really, he is biased.

I can hear the music in the background and it's like it's calling to me. Everyone is looking at me. I must have drifted off, listening to the words of the song.

Whiskey laughs. "You don't even realise how sexy as fuck you are, do you?"

I shake my head, freeing my body from this trance I feel like I'm in. "I don't dance like that to be sexy, I dance like that because it makes *me* feel sexy. I love dancing but I don't get to do it often."

"Well, you should. Would you be interested in dancing for us?" Whiskey asks as Drew squeezes my waist.

"What? Are you serious?"

"Yeah, I'm serious. I don't joke about dancing."

I don't say anything. I can't say anything because I don't know what to say. This is something I can only dream of, but I can't do it. I can't risk someone knowing who I really am.

"Wow, thank you so much. I would love to dance for you, but I can't. I'm sorry. My life is... erm... complicated."

"Okay. If you ever change your mind then just give

me a shout." She hands me her business card which has the Whiskey Sour sign on it and her phone number.

On one hand, I'm disappointed that she didn't try and convince me, but on the other hand, it makes it easier for me.

I look up at Drew and see the disappointment on his face. He leans into me. "We can talk about this later, after I've fucked you hard for making me tent in front of my friends." He pulls me closer and kisses me just below my earlobe. I truly believe that this spot is directly connected to my G-spot.

I look at Sawyer and Whiskey and then I chance my arm. "I'd love a membership though. I'd love to come back and dance again. This club feels safe. It feels like home. I know that sounds stupid, but I feel I can be who I really want to be here."

Drew speaks first. "I'll vouch for her and pay for her membership."

I touch his arm with my hand. "I can pay for it myself."

"It's seven hundred and fifty pounds a year," Sawyer says. "We can give you discount because of your relationship with Drew."

"Thanks, Sawyer, but when you get to know me, you'll know that I can pay for myself. I can do everything for myself. I don't need a man to pay for me or another one doing me favours. I don't need a man to know who I am. But I am a woman who *needs* a membership to this club."

He laughs. "Point taken. Stig will arrange a membership for you. I think we will love you dancing and enjoying yourself."

He picks up on the phone on the bar, and after pressing a number on the keypad he says, "Stig can you arrange a membership for..." He looks at me. "What's your full name?"

Shit. I don't want to give my full name. I take a deep breath "Pinkie!" I try to look confident in my new name.

He looks at me, searching for something in my eyes. I'm not sure if he sees it or not, but he says on the phone, "Pinkie." He goes quiet. "Yes Stig, just Pinkie!"

He chuckles and then hangs up. "It will be waiting for you when you leave. You just need to pay before you collect it."

"That's not a problem." I smile, thinking about all the fun I can have here in this club. I turn around to Drew with a big smile on my face. "Thank you so much for bringing me here. I love it."

"It makes me so happy to see you happy, sugar."

We sit at the bar for another half an hour or so when I look at my watch. It's four o'clock in the morning. Everyone left the club a long time ago and we've been chatting to Whiskey and all the staff.

"Oh my God, Drew. I have to go home. I can't be going in the house when everyone else is getting up." I stand up and start panicking. I'm almost running out of the club.

There is still music playing, which is strange, because all the guests have left. It's only the four of us and the dancers and bar staff. Even while I'm panicking and getting frantic, the words of the song hit me.

"Wait, sugar. Let me get you a cab. I can't have you trying to flag one down at this time in the morning," Drew says, following me to the door.

Stig walks up to me. "Are you ready for your membership, Pinkie?" he says, winking at me.

"Shit! I don't have time to get it now. I need to get home." I am really panicking. My mother and father are really early risers and I need to be tucked up in my bed with every trace of Pinkie removed from sight before they get up. "Can I... can I come tomorrow night and get it or is this a one night deal?"

He chuckles with his deep, sexy voice. "Pinkie, the way you danced out there tonight, this deal is open for a very long time."

"Thank fuck for that." I smile at him as Drew opens the door for me to go outside to the waiting cab he called for me.

I slip inside the taxi and Drew leans in and kisses

me. "One day you might tell me your real story, sugar. Will I see you tonight?"

I kiss him back. "Too right you will. I need your cock again and again until you leave me."

He smiles and then closes the door. I panic all the way home and make it into my bedroom about twenty minutes before my parents get up.

Phew, that was close. Too close.

Game Changer

I slept until two o'clock and my parents are out when I walk into the kitchen to get some food. I see a note.

We left you sleeping, but you have to start getting up earlier. You can't sleep your life away. We are out for the night and won't be back until tomorrow evening. Then we are going to sit down and have a talk about your future.

Fucking great. What am I going to do now? If they make me get a job, I won't be able to go out at night and Pinkie will have to disappear. I don't want that to happen. I love the strong, independent woman I am when I'm Pinkie. She takes no shit from anyone.

Fuck, fuck, fuck. I bang my head against the wall in sheer frustration. I stomp back up to my bedroom. I need to make a decision, but I don't know what that will be.

While I'm in the shower, I hear my phone beep with a message. After I'm dry but still wrapped in a towel, I move into the bedroom, sit on the edge of the bed, and read my message.

Hey sugar, hope everything was ok when you went home. I was worried about you – you've never run away from me before.

Bless him; he's worried I left because of him.

Never had to run away from you. I need to run to you right now though. I need you to fuck my problems away. Are you up for that?

Blunt, but to the point... typical Pinkie style.

Always ready for you sugar.

Give me half an hour and I will be knocking on your door and you better have my best friend, your cock, out ready for me.

He is at your service sugar.

I smile and throw my phone down on the floor. As

it's daytime, I need to wear a different outfit. I can't be walking around looking like a hooker all day; that only works at night.

I find a pair of black tight capri pants which I don't think I've worn before. I team it up with a bright pink bra, black blouse which I leave open to below my breast line, then I throw on a bright pink scarf I bought one day when I was shopping for Pinkie's clothes. I put on a pair of high heeled fuck me shoes and pick up my handbag. I look in the mirror and smile at the person looking back at me. I prefer this person to Jennifer; she is so boring. Pinkie makes me feel sexy, confident, alive.

Once again, I find myself on the way to The Kensington Hotel, thinking about Drew's cock. As I knock on his door, he opens it and pulls me inside then slams the door shut. He pushes me against it and kisses me furiously. It's like he's trying to eat my insides.

When he breaks away from the kiss, I smile at him. "Happy to see me, are you?" He is about to answer me when I slide down the door, grab his cock, and wrap my lips around it. He leans over me, holding himself up by placing his hands on the wall over my head.

"Oh, Pinkie. That has to be the best welcome a man can get." He pushes his cock further into my mouth until I open my throat and let it slide further in.

"Fuck!" he says, and pulls out of my mouth as I gag and splutter. I wipe my mouth with the back of my hand and stand up, placing my hands on his face, and kiss him again.

This time, I pull away and place my hands on his chest, pushing him away from me. He looks at me, confused. I smile and push him out of the way so I can reach over for the chair. He watches me as I undo my trousers, take them off, and bend over the chair.

"Now it's my turn," I say with a smile as I wiggle my naked arse in his face. "Get down there and lick my pussy until I scream out your name."

He stands there for a second before he goes down on his knees and spreads my cheeks apart. He uses his tongue to lick from my arse to my pussy. I moan as he goes. He pulls my cheeks even further apart and flicks his tongue over my clit. I flinch, and then I relax and enjoy the wave that's coming over me.

"Fuck, Drew! Fuck!" I shout as my first orgasm hits me.

He has his tongue inside my pussy and I can feel my walls squeezing it tight.

"I love your juices on my tongue. Pinkie, you are fucking amazing."

When I can breathe again, I say, "Shut up and fuck me already."

He laughs. "You are definitely not like other women. All they want is to talk. All you want is my cock." I feel him standing up.

"Hell yeah. Come on. Don't keep me wait..."

I don't even finish speaking before he has thrust the full way inside me. The angle I'm in makes it feel so much deeper and more sensitive.

"Fuck, sugar. This feels good." He stops and takes a deep breath then starts thrusting in and out as fast as he can go. Holy fuck, he is fucking me senseless.

He licks his finger and runs it down my arse as he's thrusting his cock into me. He pushes his finger into my tight hole.

It's too many feelings all at once and I just can't handle it. "Drew, I can't hold on." I feel my walls clench around his cock and finger.

"Oh my God." He is balls deep and he stops thrusting. I can feel his cock getting bigger and exploding inside me.

He falls on top of me over the chair. "That was..."

"I know," I say. Words can't describe what just happened.

He eventually climbs off me and helps me up. My back is killing me but it was so worth it.

"I'm going for a shower then we're going out for dinner."

"Sounds like a great plan. I'm not really dressed for anywhere sophisticated though."

He laughs. "I didn't get much of a chance to see

what you're wearing, sugar, but you are beautiful and don't need to worry."

"Get in that shower. I'm starving."

He chuckles and kisses me on the cheek.

I take the time that he's in the shower to reapply my makeup and make sure my hair is on properly.

We get a taxi to The Ivy. I've been here lots of times but I don't tell Drew that.

Dinner is fantastic as it always is there. When we're having coffee, I ask, "Can we go to Whiskey Sour so I can get my membership since I didn't have time last night?"

He smiles. "Of course. I know you liked it there. I can see you are definitely going to make good use of your membership when I'm gone."

"Hell yeah. Everyone is unique in their own way and they are not afraid to show the world. That's all I want. To be me. To be the *real* me."

He reaches across and puts his hand on top of mine and I feel the air change between us. "Do you want to talk about you? I know you're not Pinkie all day, every day. Who are you?'

I try to drag my hand away but he won't let me. I slowly bring my eyes up from his hand to his eyes. I can feel a tear coming, but I take a deep breath. "My life is a whole lie. During the day, I hate myself. Hate the person I am. At night, I love myself and the person I have become, but I can't be that person for the majority of the time. Today has been refreshing because I can be Pinkie for at least twenty-four hours. That is a novelty to me."

"Why do you have to hide behind this façade, even though I love it?"

"My parents are trying to marry me off to someone they choose."

He gasps. "What century are they from for fuck's sake?"

I laugh. "This one, believe it or not. They keep making me have dinner with guys who are, well, boring, but have money, or business connections, or something else that will help them. They aren't worried about me and what I want."

"You need to get the fuck away from them, sugar. That is outrageous. You can't be tamed. You shouldn't be tamed."

I smile. "Thanks, Drew. I thought that maybe I could be Pinkie for a few months until one of the men catch my eye and then I retire and put her in the attic to be found when I'm old and senile. *But,* I don't want to give her up. I would give my daytime persona up without a shadow of a doubt except it means that I have to give up Mother and Father as well and I'm not sure I'm ready for that."

He seems to be thinking. "Look, I know we haven't

defined what we're doing here, but you know I really like you."

I laugh. "More like my pussy."

He chuckles. "No. I like *you* a lot. I know we don't want a relationship, but if you want, I can put you up in a flat until you can stand on your own two feet if it helps you get away from them."

"Like a prostitute, you mean?"

His face is ashen and he starts to stutter. "No! No. God, that's not what I meant."

I laugh. "I know, and thank you. If I needed to hear that then I would be really happy right now. Just to put you straight, I have enough money to buy this restaurant and have a lot of change beside. I don't want you to ever give me money. That will just cheapen what we have. I don't want to be tied down either, and you only coming over once a month has made our relationship easier. I know you don't really want more and neither do I."

"Wow, okay. I didn't know that. I don't make commitments, Pinkie, but I would have to you."

"I really appreciate it, but when I do make a commitment with a man, I don't want it to be a once a month kind of thing. I want the fire in my belly to burn me up inside. I want passion and I want a man who is going to be here for me."

He takes my hand from underneath his and brings

it to his lips. "Thank you for giving me your time when I am here. It really does mean so much to me. You're right. You deserve someone who will love you with an intensity that you crave. I am not that man."

"I know that, but it's been fun while it's lasted. Let's have this weekend and then see what happens after that. My parents want to talk to me tomorrow and I can see that my life is going to change drastically. I'm going to have to give up one of my lives and I'm not sure which one will win."

He stands and pulls out my chair and then takes my hand and we leave the restaurant and jump into the taxi which is waiting for us. I'm really excited about going to Whiskey Sour again, but I'm also sad as I know in my heart that this weekend will be mine and Drew's last weekend together.

As soon as we walk inside Whiskey Sour, I can feel the electricity in the air. This place has a sense of home; a sense of excitement like I've never experienced before. Stig greets us at the door and he has a big smile on his face when he sees me. He hugs me.

He stands back and reaches into the office. "I have your paperwork. Are you ready to join the club?"

I laugh. "More than ever!" We spend the next ten

minutes going over the paperwork and then he hands me my own Whiskey Sour membership card. He then opens the door, and once again, I'm surprised at how much noise that door suppresses from the club. The buzz is electric, and I stand, transfixed on the stage. This time the theme is disco dancing. I learned the last time I was here that disco is Wanda's speciality, and with her fluorescent legwarmers and day glo net gloves, her neon yellow underwear and big hair, she is the epitome of an eighties chick.

I feel Drew's hand on the lower part of my back as he guides me over to a table near the bar. He sits me down while I continue to stare. He chuckles as he moves to the bar to order a drink for me.

When he returns, I can't focus on him, only on the girl dancing on the stage. She has so much energy, her body moving along with the fast music. I really want to dance with her.

I clap wildly when she's finished and the lights go dark. I turn to Drew for the first time since we arrived here. "She is fabulous, isn't she?" I take a sip of my drink.

He smiles. "She sure is, but you are much better."

I laugh. "You're just saying that because you want to get into my panties."

He nods his head. "I sure do. I have to stock up on Pinkie fucks before I go home."

"When are you going home?"

"Tomorrow afternoon, so tonight is our last night, sugar."

"Then let's make sure we don't stay here really late so that we can spend it together. I can stay tonight if that's okay, and then I have that stupid meeting with my parents tomorrow evening."

"Oh yeah. Make sure you let me know how that goes."

"I will." I laugh. "But I don't want to talk about this now. Let's just have fun."

The next dancer is Jeannie. I recognise her because she is Stig's girlfriend. She is really nice and she keeps him on his toes. The light focuses on her in the centre of the stage and she starts to shake some large feather fans in front of her. The chords to *A Guy Who Takes His Time* play.

I stare at her. Her top is made out of strings of pearls which are denser around her breasts, and a pair of pearl panties. The rest of the strings just hang. It is so sexy.

As she dances around the stage, she is being very coy, yet at the same time, she manages to lose her bra top and her panties.

She has the fans back up now and she ends the song on a note where she has the fans up in the air and she is showing everything she has. It's only for a split second and then the lights go dark.

I clap like a mad woman and then turn to have another drink. I don't know how many I've had, but I'm having a ball.

The lights come on and then the DJ starts to play music and some of the customers get up to dance.

"Can I...?"

I don't have to finish as Drew says, "Go dance, sugar."

I kiss him deeply and then walk over to the dance floor. As the music changes, I remember last night when the music was talking to me, and my interlude in the corridor. I hadn't really thought about it as I rushed away last night. I start to feel hot when I remember the heat of the mystery man, how he made me feel in seconds.

The music changes when I get on the dance floor. I sway a little until I hear the beat. I love this song. *Every Breath You Take* by the Police.

I giggle to myself. I must be going daft if I think every song is about me. The music is hypnotic. I close my eyes and move to it. I lose myself in it. I smile, my eyes closed as I move. I fist pump my arm in the air as I jump up and down. I open my eyes and look around me; people are dancing next to me. Everyone is having a good time, but I feel like someone is watching me. It feels good.

The next song is even better. *Everybody's Free* by Rozalla.

A real hit with the audience by the looks of it as everyone starts shaking their arses and moving in time to the music.

I think I might have had too much to drink. I shake my head, laughing. I'm going to risk going to the toilet; surely I won't get accosted a second time. I'm not sure how I feel about that because I enjoyed it the last time.

As I push the door open into the corridor, I look out and see no one is around. As I approach the toilet door, I hear another door open and someone coming up behind me.

"Don't turn around!" The deep voice booms and sends twitches all the way to my pussy.

"Why should I listen to you?"

"Because you haven't turned around yet. You like playing this game." He is behind me now; I can feel the heat of his body as he pushes me against the wall. "You came back for more? Did you think of me last night when Drew was inside you? I thought of you when I was inside my hook up."

I laugh at him. "So you thought of me when you were fucking someone else and you think you can tell me this because...?"

"I know you want me as much as I want you. I can feel it. Your pulse is hammering in your neck. I can smell your excitement right now." He leans down and takes a deep breath. "Gorgeous. I bet you taste as good as you smell." He licks my neck and then blows air on it. It makes me shiver. "See, your goose bumps, all your movements, show me how much you're enjoying our stolen moments.."

"Just because you know how to turn a girl on, doesn't mean she wants you."

"So, you are turned on? I knew it. I haven't thought of anything else since I tasted your lips. I want to taste them again." He pushes himself up against me and I can feel the full length of his cock. My legs clench together.

Again, he covers my eyes and turns my head so that my lips are accessible to him. He licks my bottom lip, and then he breathes on it. He kisses me. I try not to open my lips, I really do, but I just can't help myself. My body is reacting to him, even if my mind isn't. I want this man with all my being. I want him. His tongue forces its way inside my mouth; it's hot and furious as it searches for my tongue. I relent and my tongue fights with his. Then he pulls away.

"Just perfect," he whispers in my ear. He still has his hand over my eyes, but I can smell him. I'll recognise his scent anywhere now. He turns me to face the wall again. He leans down and has his mouth next to my ear.

"God, you're unbelievable. I was drawn to you when you first arrived." He snakes his hand around my waist and he starts to put it down the front of my trousers.

"What? What are you doing?"

His mouth is almost inside my ear. "I want to know how wet you are. I want to taste you on my fingers."

I relax and let him continue. This feels really naughty, but really nice at the same time.

"What if someone comes? What if they see us here?"

"The only person coming is you." He growls into my ear as he slides his hand down the front of my panties and his finger hits my clit.

"Oh my God, that feels good. Don't stop. I don't care if anyone sees us. It feels too good."

"You're a dirty bitch. I love it." He runs his finger between my lips and then he pushes one finger inside.

I take a deep breath. "Please..."

"God, you're tight. What do you want me to do now?" he says, stilling his finger assault.

"More ..."

He chuckles and he takes his finger out and then thrusts two inside. He presses himself against my back, making me flat to the wall. He moves my hips out slightly so that he can move his fingers in and out. I can feel the full length of his cock against me and I move my hips against it.

"You are such a tease, Pinkie," he says, thrusting deeper and harder. "I can't wait to have my cock squeezed by these walls."

It takes me a minute but I realise he said my name. "How... how do you know who I am?"

"Do you think I would just randomly attack women in this corridor? No. I know who you are. Everyone who works here knows who you are. We've seen you dancing and we know that you are going to end up working here. The way men react to your body is the stuff wet dreams are made of."

I try to squirm, but it doesn't work. If anything, it just feels so much better.

He kisses me on the neck then bites my earlobe. "God, you do things to me that I didn't know could be done."

I'm panting as his thumb starts to rub my clit. "I want to know who you are. Please?"

"You will, in due course. I know you have a membership, but just so you know you won't be bringing another man here. Once Drew goes home, you're mine."

I try to protest, but each movement I make to get

away from him brings the moment of orgasm closer. "You're a bastard. Take your hands off me."

He laughs and then starts to pull his hand away, but he knew I was going to grab it and push it right back down. "Don't you dare do that until you finish me off. I'm so close. I need it. Please?"

"Anything for you, duchess. Anything you want." He increases the speed of his fingers and, at the same time, he's gyrating his hips against me so his cock is rubbing against my back. It is sensation overload and I know I'm getting close. I groan as the familiar waves wash over me. I stop breathing for a moment as my body shakes with the intensity of my orgasm.

"That was the most beautiful thing I've seen, watching you topple over the edge under my touch. Duchess, I can't wait for Drew to leave. I'll be waiting. I'll be ready for you."

I can't speak.

He removes his hand and then he puts them in his mouth. "Like pure honey. Better than I thought it would taste." He kisses me once more on the neck, just where my pulse is.

"See you next time, Pinkie. I'll be waiting, not very patiently."

He disappears again and I'm left frustrated, but I've only myself to blame really as I could have turned around.

After I've finally managed to go to the toilet, I feel like I've sobered up a lot. Time for more drink.

When I walk back into the club, I go straight over to Drew. "You were gone a while." He grabs my waist and pulls me closer. I feel a little bit guilty, but then again, I know Drew and I are going our separate ways tomorrow.

When I think about tomorrow, I think about my parents, and I wonder what they want to talk about. I get a feeling of dread, but quickly shake it off. I want to enjoy the rest of my time with Drew.

"Are you enjoying the show, Drew?"

"I sure am, sugar, but I'm looking forward to later more." He pulls me in for a kiss, his hand on my arse.

When he pulls back, I move over to my chair to sip my drink and think about what happened in the corridor.

The lights go down and the music starts and I, once again, lose myself in the world of burlesque. Halfway through, I say to Drew, "I'm going to get a drink. Do you want one?"

"Stay there, sugar. I'll get it."

"It's okay. I want to stretch my legs and I might look at the cocktail menu and choose something different. I feel like a change." I slip off my chair and kiss him on my way past. Everything feels different and I don't like it.

"Hey, Pinkie," Spence says as I approach the bar.

I look at him and wonder if it's him. Then I see him watching Snow dancing on the stage and I know he doesn't have eyes for anyone else.

"Hey, Spence. I'm looking for the cocktail menu if you have one."

"We sure do. Hang on, I'll get you one."

I turn around and lean on the bar so I can look out. I carefully look around the club. I don't know who I'm looking for but I'm hoping my body will know when.

It's hard to see because it's so dark, but then my eye catches sight of a man sitting at one of the front tables. He's leaning back in his chair, watching me. There is no one else at his table, no spare drink or anything; he has to be on his own.

He catches my eye and he nods his head at me and then he looks away. No, not my man. He would keep staring.

I laugh at myself. My man! I turn back to the bar and Spence hands me the cocktail menu.

"So, what do you think about the place?" he asks, while I look at the pictures of the drinks.

"I love it. Snow is so graceful and alluring," I say, looking over my shoulder.

He's staring at her. "Yes, she is. She is an unbelievable dancer and she had given up on dancing, but when you're that good, you just can't stop." I can see by looking at him that he's madly in love with her.

"I got my membership today," I tell him. "Drew is going home tomorrow and I wanted to be able to come on my own. Now that I've met you guys, I won't feel awkward or anything."

He laughs. "We are one big family here and you are very welcome. I know we would love for you to work here too."

"Thank you. I might think about it, but I have a few things I need to sort out first."

"That would be great. I think you would fit in well. Now, have you decided on a cocktail?"

I laugh. "Yes. Please can I have a Pina Colada? I feel like something tropical."

"Of course you can. I'll get Drew his drink too." He moves off to make the drinks.

I turn around and lean my elbows on the bar behind me so I can see the stage. Sage is doing her GI Jane routine; she is scary but so sexy.

While I'm watching her, I notice someone watching me. I turn my head and see a man at the bar. He is about six feet two inches. He has long hair tied back in a man bun. He has tattoos all down his arms and I can see them on his chest at the top of his t-shirt. He is mesmerizing. His face is chiselled, with a dimple in his chin. He smiles at me and his teeth are as dazzling as his smile. It sends ripples through my body. I blush and look to the floor. I then look back at the stage, trying to ignore the burning gaze of the man.

I can hear Spence behind me, making my drinks and talking to the guy. "Good set tonight, Nate. Great crowd."

He doesn't say anything, but I'm guessing he must have nodded his head. I see him walk away from the bar with a drink in his hand, and just before he moves into the crowd, he turns around and winks at me. Surely that isn't my mystery man. It couldn't be, could it?

Spence clears his throat to get my attention. "You okay, Pinkie?"

"Yeah, I was just... erm... captivated with Sage. She is really ballsy," I say as I turn around to smile at him.

"She sure is. I think you could give her a run for her money though."

I laugh out loud. "I'm not so sure about that."

I pay for the drinks and take them back over to Drew. I sit on the chair next to him and put my hand on his thigh. He turns to me and then leans in and kisses me. I can't help but compare his kiss to the mystery man. I thought Drew's kisses were like a drug, but ten minutes in the corridor with a stranger has made me realise that it is the same as any other kiss. Now I've had the stranger's kiss, no other will do.

Drew whispers in my ear, "Do you want to go back to the hotel? We've got all night to say goodbye."

"I want to watch the finale. Is that okay?"

"Of course it is, sugar. I love that you like this place. I really enjoy watching you dance. You need to reconsider, you know?"

"I really like it here too and I'd love to dance here, but my life is too complicated. I don't know what my parents are going to say tomorrow. They might tell me to get my act together, or they might say that they have someone that they're marrying me off to."

"They wouldn't do that really, would they?"

"Yes, they would, and I really believe that's what they're going to say. I want to enjoy tonight. It might be my last night of freedom."

"Then we stay until they throw us out. You don't have to be home until tomorrow afternoon so we can stay as late as we want."

"You're flying home at lunchtime though."

"I can sleep on the plane, sugar. I always do when I've spent the weekend with you. You wear me out." He takes my face in his hands and gently kisses me. His tongue penetrates my lips and he moans.

I pull back and take a sip of my drink. I don't look at Drew; my feelings are all over the place. Luckily, the girls keep us entertained and I enjoy the show. When it's time for them to do their freestyle section, I get excited.

Everyone is quiet. The lights are dark. I can hear the girls getting ready on the stage. I wonder if they really don't know what's going to be played. Maybe if I come more often, I'll notice a pattern of the songs played. I wonder what it's going to be tonight.

The first few beats play and then I hear Madonna's voice. *Like A Prayer*. I love this song. I watch the girls as they all dance a different dance to the same beat. It really is a fantastic sight.

I don't know where to look.

There's a standing ovation when it's over. We watch Baby and Dee Dee doing their set and then the finale begins.

There should have been fireworks it was that spectacular. Whoever puts it all together is a genius.

I dance some more until all the customers leave and then I move over to the bar where Drew is sitting with Sawyer and Whiskey.

He doesn't see me coming up behind him, but I hear him say, "I know, Sawyer. I've got feelings for her but I know nothing can come of it. We are from different worlds. She's ready to move on and I know I have to let her go. I'm not saying it won't hurt, but it makes me happy. She is a much better person now than when I first met her."

Sawyer nods his head to me and Drew turns around. He smiles one of his big smiles and opens his arms for me to walk into them. He pulls me close and kisses me. "Hey, sugar. Let's have another drink and then we can go."

"I like that idea. Can I have a raspberry Cosmopolitan?"

Spence makes my drink. "Can you get one for everyone, please?" I ask.

He looks at me. "Are you sure?"

I nod. "Make sure everyone gets one, including you."

He smiles and walks away to make the drinks for all the girls and the rest of the staff who are left behind. Snow walks behind the bar to give him a kiss. His whole face lights up as he pulls her in tight.

I hear a deep voice booming from behind me. "God, get a room, will you?" It sends chills through me. My body is on high alert; I'm sure this is the voice that has been talking to me in the corridor.

My mind is racing. Do I want to turn around and find out who it is? What if it spoils my fantasy? I feel him moving closer. How does someone make me feel this way?

He is right behind me. I try to look into the mirror behind the bar, but he's being hidden by the bottles on the shelves.

He leans on the bar next to me and I still don't want to look... I'm scared.

He leans closer. I can feel him moving towards my face. "Hi, duchess," he says, reaching out his hand. "Thanks for the drink. Next time I hope you let me drink it off your body," he whispers into my ear.

I gasp. If I thought I was in control of my body then I was sadly mistaken. This man, whoever he is, is controlling my reactions. I need to turn and see who he is, even though I think I know.

"Aren't you going to look at me? Do you not want to see the next man who is going to feed off your body like it's his last meal?"

Oh... my... God. I hesitate then I very slowly turn. I see his arms first. They are covered in tattoos. I turn again slightly and he has a *very* tight t-shirt on which is stretched across his toned chest. I see the tattoos at the top of his chest. I know who he is, but I'm still savouring every single moment of soaking him up before looking at his face.

When I have turned around fully to take all of him in, I gasp. Up close, he is gorgeous. Absolutely fucking gorgeous!

He smiles at me and his teeth are perfect. His dimple is showing and his hair is long, but tied back. He holds out his hand. "Hi. I'm Nate," he says, a little bit louder. Then he whispers, "You're mine. When I felt you fall apart earlier, I knew I had to have you. I want you in my bed, Pinkie."

I take his hand and shake it, squeezing his fingers at the same time. He smiles at my attempt to get the upper hand. "I'm Pinkie. Pleased to meet you, *Nate!*" I spit out his name. I try to take my hand back but he grips it firmly until I look up into his eyes again.

"Now, now. You could be nicer to the guy who just gave you an Earth-shattering orgasm," he says, lowering his voice.

I blush. He lets go of my hand and then shakes his head. He leans over again and says into my ear, "Just watching you blush is making me hard."

I know I shouldn't, but I can't help myself. I look down at his crotch and see the outline of his cock. He takes his hand, and before adjusting himself, he squeezes it to show me how large and thick it really is. He laughs as my blush deepens.

I look back up at him and I don't know whether I like him or if he really pisses me off. One thing I am one hundred percent sure of is that he really, *really* turns me on.

"Let me help you carry those drinks," he says, louder for everyone else to hear, and he starts picking up the glasses and takes them to everyone. I stare at him. I have never met anyone so cocksure. I don't know whether I find it arrogant or sexy as hell. I have a little giggle and then take the drinks to Drew and Whiskey.

We all sit around one of the larger tables and everyone is talking about the dances tonight. I look around this table and everyone is so different; they come from different corners of England and they all seem such good friends. I don't have friends like these and I'm slightly envious. Nate sits down next to me, of course, and I can feel him looking at me.

Every now and again, he brushes my arm. It looks like an accident but I'm starting to believe it's not. We talk about the music tonight and then I remember he's the DJ. Everything starts to make sense. The music talking to me last night, the feeling that my mystery man was trying to tell me something.

"So, Pinkie," he says. "What do you think of Whiskey Sour?"

Everyone turns to look at me expectantly.

I smile. "I love it." His hand drops onto my thigh while I'm talking. It's hard to concentrate. I look at him then I turn quickly away as I realise I'm blushing. "I bought my membership tonight." His hand very slowly moves up my thigh, inching closer to my heat. "I just can't believe I haven't been here before." I rush through the last bit so I can take a deep breath to try and still my erratic heartbeat.

"That's fantastic," he says. "Now you can come as

often you want." He winks at me. He freaking winks at me and it takes all the self-control I have not to jump his bones right here, right now, in front of all these people.

Luckily the attention is taken off me when Whiskey asks Drew, "When are you coming back?"

"I'm not sure. I'm going to work on your promotional package, but I have a few things going on in the States that I need to deal with desperately. I've been over here more than normal this year." He turns to look at me and smiles.

Sawyer laughs. "I know. We didn't think we would ever get rid of you."

Nate's hand is now between my thighs and he's skimming his finger over my lips. I can feel the heat and wetness pooling in my knickers. I look everywhere except at him. I squeeze my legs closed, trapping his hand, hoping the tingling will go away. He chuckles and I glare at him. He smiles back.

I need to get myself under control. I reach down and take his hand from between my legs and place it on his. Before I can take my hand away, he manages to swap so that his hand is on top of mine and then he runs it up his leg until he reaches his cock, which is hard as a rock.

He wraps my hand around it and squeezes my hand so I can really feel it. It jumps under my touch and I gasp. Drew looks at me and I blush. I manage to pull my hand away from Nate's cock and then I push my chair back.

"I'm just going to the toilet. I'll be back in a bit. Don't leave without me, please!"

He pulls me in close and kisses my lips gently. "Why would I do that? You have a date with my cock tonight."

I laugh and it is just the thing I need to break the tension. Without turning back to look at Nate, I hurry across the club to the nearest toilet. I use the disabled toilet and close the door behind me. I lean up against it and slide to the floor. What the fuck does Nate thinks he's doing? Who does he think he is? He can't just touch me like that and expect me to touch him; I don't even know him. I'm appalled, but at the same time, so turned on by it. I just don't know what is happening to me. He must do that to all the women in the club. He's a fucking player and I'm letting him play me.

I get back up and splash my face with water. When I look in the mirror, I see a flushed woman looking back at me. I realise that during those few minutes when he was touching me and making me touch him, I felt alive.

"God, what is wrong with me? Why did I let him get to me?" I say to my reflection as I shake my head.

I take a deep breath and open the door to go and join everyone else. As soon as it's halfway open, someone pushes it from the other side. Before I even look up, I know who that someone is.

"What the fuck...?" I don't get to finish my sentence before Nate has pushed me against the wall and closed the door behind him.

"Shh, duchess," He silences me with a mouth-watering, knicker-wetting, body-tingling kiss. My body presses into his as his tongue invades my mouth with such force I feel like I'm melting into the wall.

He has one hand behind my head, tipping it so he can get better access to my mouth. His other hand is at the base of my spine, pulling my body into his.

We both moan and then he slows down his assault. Before I can speak, he puts his finger over my mouth. "Don't say anything, please. I know you're probably pissed off, but I just wanted another taste of you. I want you badly and I'm going to get you. You're going to be mine, duchess."

No one tells me to be quiet. "Why do you think I want to be yours? Don't I get a choice in this matter?"

He laughs. "Feisty. I knew you were feisty. Your kiss tells me how much you want me. I can't wait to sink my cock into your wet pussy and hear you screaming for more."

I laugh. "So sure of yourself, aren't you? Well, I'm leaving soon with Drew. He is taking me back to his place. I'm staying the night there. So think about that while your cock pines for me!"

I push past him and go to open the door. He moves quickly and blocks it. He laughs. "I told you before, you will be mine, and if you need to sleep with a wrinkly cock then off you go and enjoy it. It will be the last time you will have another cock that isn't mine. I'll be waiting for you."

I don't know what to say. He is pissing me off but turning me on at the same time. "God, you make me so angry."

He laughs at me. As he puts his hand on the door handle, he says, "I bet you think of me when you come tonight. I know I'll be thinking of you."

He opens the door and lets me walk through. I'm in a daze.

When I get back to Drew, I tell him it's time to leave. I don't want Nate to come back while I'm still here. We say goodbye to everyone, and just as we get to the door, I hear the music change to U2's *With or Without You*. I smile to myself.

We get back to the Kensington Hotel and I'm kissing Drew in the lift. Things are starting to get out of control. "Slow down, sugar. We've got all night."

I don't listen to him. I pull him down to his room, and as soon as he has the door open, I take my clothes off in a rush as I stride towards the bed. When I'm completely naked, I climb up on the bed, and on all fours, I turn my head to look at him and say, "Drew, fuck me like it's the last thing you are ever going to do. I want it hard, fast, and brutal!"

He starts to take his clothes off slowly.

I don't have the patience. "Drew, now!"

He laughs and then climbs up behind me, slams into me, and says, "Yes m'lady!"

He drives me hard, brutal, and quickly, but it's not enough. I need to orgasm and I can't. Fucking Nate. I fucking hate him. He's done this to me. He's made me not long for Drew's touch anymore. All I want is for him to touch me with those muscly, tattooed arms. Kiss me with his sumptuous lips. Fuck me with that rigid cock.

I can feel myself getting to the point of no return. Drew says, "I'm close, sugar."

I imagine Nate behind me, riding me and slapping my arse. It sends me over the top, and then I feel Drew joining me.

We both collapse on the bed. I feel guilty, but satisfied.

"Fuck, sugar. That was the best yet." He climbs off the bed and I follow him. I put my clothes on and he watches me. "Where are you going? I thought you were staying with me tonight."

"I know, but I need to go home. I'm worried about what my parents are going to talk to me about and I need to think about what I want to do." I kiss him, and he drops his hand down to my arse.

"This feels like goodbye, Pinkie. What's happened? What's changed?"

"A lot feels like it's changed, Drew. It is goodbye. Let me know you get home safe like you always do. Please?"

He kisses me again and then pulls me into a hug, holding me tight. "Of course I will. If you ever need anything, just let me know. You know I'm here for you whenever."

"I know. Thank you."

I walk out of his hotel room, and when the door closes in the lift, I cry. I lean my head against the mirror and Nate pops into my mind.

I can't stop thinking of him. He was right; I did think of him when I came.

I'm fucked.

Pinkie Becomes a Reality

When I get home, I'm still crying. I feel so emotional; I don't know what's wrong with me. I crawl into my own bed and think about how my life has changed in the last six months.

Drew was a big inspiration for Pinkie. He nurtured me and let me be the person who was inside, screaming to be let out. Since I've been Pinkie, I've been the happiest I've been in years. My parents make me feel suppressed and unhappy. I'm dreading whatever they're going to say tonight when they get home.

My mind turns to Nate. I hate him, but I want him. He makes my body respond to him in seconds. My body wants him. He is frustrating and domineering and I don't like that. I always like to be in charge of my own destiny, and for someone to tell me I'm going to be his makes me want to rebel and prove that I won't be made to do something I don't want to do.

On the other hand, I crave his touch. I want to know that his eyes are watching me. Wanting me.

When I wake, it's four o'clock, and my parents are due back in an hour. I shower and get dressed and I'm sitting in the kitchen with a cup of strong coffee when they arrive.

As usual, I'm wearing my boring beige clothes with my flat loafers. I wonder if Nate would want me if he could see me like this. I very much doubt it. How can I even contemplate a relationship with anyone when I know that I can't be real to myself, either as Pinkie or as Jennifer?

Mother comes over and kisses me on the cheek. "Hello, darling. How was your weekend?" She pauses for a second, not waiting for me to answer. "Your father and I had great fun, didn't we, darling?"

"Yes, dear," he mutters.

"We played boules, bridge, and..."

I tune out because I don't need to know what they did. They go to the same place and do the same thing all the time.

"Jennifer?"

Crap. I wasn't listening and she's looking at me for an answer to whatever questions she just asked me.

"Sorry, Mother. What was that?"

She sighs with exasperation. "Did you do anything nice while we were away?" She is standing in front of me with her hands on her hips. I see Father trying to sneak out of the kitchen door when she looks up and says, "Leonard!" He stops and walks back into the kitchen then sits down next to me.

I guess there is no beating around the bush; this conversation is happening now.

"I met some friends, did a bit of shopping and then went for a few drinks. Nothing special."

She sits down on the other side of me. "Jennifer, we know you've been sneaking out almost every night for the last few months. Are you seeing someone?"

I blush. I wonder if they know about Pinkie too. That would be embarrassing.

"No, I'm not seeing anyone. How do you know?"

She shakes her head as if she is embarrassed by me. If only she knew the full story.

"I heard a noise one night, and when I went into your bedroom, you were gone. I waited until I saw the lights of the taxi at the end of the drive. I checked again a couple of nights later and you weren't there."

"Why didn't you ask me about it then, Mother?"

"I was hoping you would talk to me about it. Something must be wrong for you to feel that you need to sneak out."

"Did you ever see me sneak out or come back in?"

I'm worried now she saw Pinkie coming back in and not Jennifer.

"No," she says, shaking her head. "As soon as I saw the lights on the taxi, I went to bed and just listened to you coming up the stairs and closing your bedroom door."

"You've been putting me under pressure to meet someone so that I can get married. I don't agree with that. I believe that true love can only be found naturally and it can't be forced on a couple. I want to find my one true love, not have him forced upon me. I want to choose a man for myself, someone who is going to love and respect me, not one who is trying to please my parents. I can't do it, Mother." The tears are forming now and I'm trying desperately not to let them overflow, but she needs to know how I feel about this.

"Our families have always had marriages of convenience. Not all of them have turned out as well as mine and your father's, but most of them do. It works well for business reasons and for the family."

"But where does love come into all of this?" I shout.

"Love is not everything, Jennifer. Love does not make the world go round. Love does not build bigger and better businesses."

"That might be true, but I am not a business you can buy or sell. I am a human being who wants to fall in love with the right person, and I want to experiment and find that person. I know he won't be the first man that comes along, but I want to enjoy the process of finding him. I don't want the process of you finding someone that suits the family and not me."

I stand and pace the kitchen.

She bangs her fist on the table. "Sit back down, Jennifer. Now!"

Mother doesn't normally shout, so now I'm scared. I park my arse right back on my seat.

"Your father and I have had a long discussion and we have decided to give you six months before you *will* marry a man of our choosing. There is no leeway on this, Jennifer. We are giving you a chance to have as much fun as you need to have before giving your life for your family."

I stare at her. She hasn't listened to anything I just said.

"What if I don't want to marry someone you choose? What if I hate him? Are you going to make me live with someone, have sex with someone and be with them for the rest of my unhappy and miserable life?"

"Yes, that's what we're saying," Father says quietly.

I take a moment to think about what they said. "What happens if I don't marry someone after the six months? What happens then? You can't force me."

"As much as it would hurt us, we would have to cut

you off. We won't be able to support you financially and you won't be able to live in this house. Those are our rules, Jennifer, and you will abide by them," Mother says, without any hesitation or remorse.

"Well, if I have six months to live my life the way I choose, then I'm moving out tomorrow. I will find somewhere to live and then I'll go and look for a job, because at the end of the six months, I won't be coming back."

"If you decide now that you won't do as we ask at the end of the six months then we will cut you off financially now!"

"You wouldn't do that to your own flesh and blood. Would you? Seriously?"

She looks at me with what I can only describe as hatred in her eyes. I don't know why she hates me so much. I know I'm being defiant, but I would think that that shows my character and determination to be my own person. Obviously, she doesn't like that.

She looks at me with a cold stare, and with no emotion in her voice, she says, "Yes. We have built this family and business through generations and we are not going to have our futures ruined because you want to run around pretending to be someone you're not!"

Shit. She knows about Pinkie. How the fuck does she know that?

"I can't believe you would disown me because I

won't marry someone you pick. This isn't the dark ages." I can feel tears coming to my eyes.

"Well, you'd better start believing it. You can move out, you can have your fun, find a little job, and then you can come back here and marry someone we choose. If you think you can outsmart us by saying you will marry someone we choose and then not come back, you are very much mistaken." She reaches down into her bag and pulls out an envelope which contains a document. She slams it down on the table and says, "You will sign this document, and if you don't come back then you will be liable to pay back every single pound that you have spent in that six months."

I stand up. "You have got to be kidding me. You seriously expect me to sign that... that piece of shit!"

"Jennifer!" My father shouts. He hates me swearing, but seriously, is he complaining about it right now?

"What?" I can't believe this is happening to me. "You want to shout at me because I'm fucking swearing, yet you sit there quiet as a mouse and let her talk to me like that and agree that I need to sign that piece of crap she threw on the table. When did you lose your balls?"

"Don't you speak to your father like that. You can take that agreement to your room, read it, and then sign it, or you can get out and never come back. Your choice," Mother says then gets up and walks out of the kitchen.

I look at my father and he hangs his head as he shakes it from side to side. "Why couldn't you just have stayed our little Jennifer? Why did you have to want more? Why did you want to fall in love?" He gets up and walks away without waiting for me to answer him.

I flop down in the chair and rest my head in my hands. What happened to make my life so shit?

It's gone dark by the time I get up from the table and slowly make my way to my room, with the stupid agreement in my hand.

I throw myself on my bed and lie there, looking at the ceiling. What am I going to do?

I pick up my phone and ring Scottie. He's always able to put a smile on my face.

"Hey, sexy. Who are you doing?"

I laugh. "Can't you just say hi and ask how I am?"

"That is my way of asking you how you are." He laughs.

"I'm not good." I'm choked up. "Something really bad has happened. I need you to cheer me up."

"What happened, babe?"

"Can I come over? Tell Ryan I'm sorry, but I need to see you."

"Of course you can, babe. Just come over anytime. Will you be okay?"

"I'll be over within the hour and then I'll tell you everything. One more thing. Can I stay on your couch tonight?"

"No, but you can stay in the spare room. Hurry up and get over here. I'm seriously worried about you."

"See you soon, Scottie. Just so you know, it won't be Pinkie coming over, it'll be me. Jennifer."

"You'll always be Pinkie. See you soon."

I hang up and start packing my case. I make sure I pack Pinkie. I'm not ready to give up her. I take the agreement and sign it. I know I should read it before I sign it, but I take it with me downstairs and leave it on the kitchen table. Well, actually I leave the signed page. I'm taking the rest with me to show Ruby. She's a lawyer and she can help me get out of the agreement at a later date.

I take the envelope it was in and leave a note to my parents.

Fuck you. See you in six months
Jennifer

I don't even turn around when I walk out of the door. This house makes me feel sick to my stomach. I stick my middle finger up to the front door on my way down the drive to the waiting taxi.

By the time I get to Scottie's, I'm a quivering mess. I ring the bell, and when he opens the door, I almost fall through it into his arms. He doesn't miss a beat, he just hugs me and leads me into the lounge. Ryan is there and he hands me a neat vodka. They are both silent, waiting for me to speak first.

On my second vodka, I start to calm down enough to tell them what has happened.

"My real name is Jennifer Hamilton Wade. I live a privileged life, or at least I did before tonight. My parents are very old-fashioned, but they are extremely rich. Our family business has been around for generations, and recently I found out that my parents want to marry me off to someone they choose because of his financial status. They don't care that I won't know him, or that I won't love him. It means nothing to them. I mean nothing to them."

"Fuckers!" Scottie says. "Do they think this is *Downton Abbey* or something?"

I giggle in spite of everything that's going on. "I know. It's laughable."

I dig into my bag, take out the agreement, and pass it over to him.

"I want Ruby to look over it. Do you think she would?"

"Of course she would. She would do anything for you, you know that. So, how have you left it?"

"I signed the agreement, which effectively buys me six months to try and get out of it. In the meantime, I need to get a job and find somewhere to live. At the moment, I have my bank account and savings at my disposal, but whatever I spend I have to pay back immediately if I don't go home and marry the guy they choose."

"Wow," Ryan says. "So let me get this straight. They want you to marry some rich fucker whether you like him or not? Nice parents you have there, Pinkie."

"I know. Now I know why they say you can pick your friends but not your family."

"So, what are you going to do for work?" Scottie asks. "I'm sure I can get you some hours in my shop."

"Thanks, Scottie, but I've already been offered a job. I just didn't think I needed a job so I might just have to grovel and see if they will offer it to me again."

"Ooh, tell me more!" he says, pouring me another vodka.

"You know Drew was here this weekend? Well, he took me to Whiskey Sour."

"No freaking way. We've been trying to get in there for the last twelve months. It's really exclusive and they don't just let anyone in."

"I know, and it is fucking amazing. It's everything

they say and more." I take a quick drink and try not to think about Nate. I don't have room in my head for him at the moment.

"Anyway," I continue, "in between the show, they played music and I got up and danced and I lost myself in the music. It was speaking to me. I know that sounds strange, but it was."

"I've seen you dance, babe, and I bet all the men were creaming themselves." He laughs.

"You could say that. When I stopped, everyone was looking at me. I went over to Drew and he was talking to Whiskey, you know, the owner. She offered me a job, dancing at Whiskey Sour. Can you fucking believe it?"

"So, what are we waiting for? Get over there now."

"I can't. Not looking like this. I'm a mess and she offered Pinkie a job, not Jennifer."

"We wouldn't get in anyway. You need to be a member," Ryan says.

I start laughing. "Guess what I bought yesterday?"

"You didn't buy a fucking membership, did you?"

I smile. "Yes, I most certainly did."

Ryan jumps up and down like a child.

"What the fuck, Ryan?" I say, laughing.

"Seriously, Pinkie. This is epic. You have to take us with you at least once!"

"I don't know how many I can bring in on my

membership. I'll ring them and find out and then we can go. I'll ask if I can get to see Whiskey too." I yawn. "I'm worn out tonight though. Can we do it tomorrow? I need to find somewhere to live tomorrow and I need to see Ruby. I'll ring Whiskey Sour tomorrow evening and see what I can find out."

"Okay, babe. We've had enough excitement tonight. You know where the spare room is, don't you?"

I nod and hug Scottie. "Thank you. Thank you for being my friend."

"No problem. See you in the morning." He kisses me on the cheek and they head to their room.

I swig the rest of my drink and turn the light out before going into Scottie's spare room.

When I lie down, I think about everything that has happened today, yet I can still smile.

I have my friends.

I have Pinkie.

I have faith.

I have six months.

Where the fuck is she? I really thought she would be back tonight as soon as she got rid of Drew.

Maybe I read her body wrong. No, definitely not. Her body wanted me, even if she didn't know it yet. I don't know what's wrong with me. I never chase women. I don't need to chase them; they come to me in droves. The only decisions I have is which one gets to take me home. I never bring them to my place. They are transient in my life so they don't need to see where or how I live.

Pinkie is a different kettle of fish. She makes me want more. Fuck, I'm turning into a pussy.

The girls are doing great on the stage tonight, but my eyes are wandering, searching. I know she isn't here; I would have seen her from my vantage point in my booth. I can see everyone coming in, everyone on the dance floor, and everyone at the bar.

Last night was so much fun. I loved teasing her, testing her. I know I told her to go to Drew, but it killed me knowing that he was going to be the one to have her in his bed. She told me she was staying the night with him. That isn't what I wanted to hear, but I couldn't let her see how much she affected me. I want to be the only one who fucks her. No one else is going to get near her while she's in here, that's for sure.

If she comes back.

I put on the standard set of music for the break and walk over to the bar.

"Hey, Nate. Good crowd in here tonight!" Spence says as he pours me a drink. I don't need to tell him what I want; he already knows.

"Yeah, not bad for a Sunday night." I lean against the bar, looking out towards the door.

He watches me. "You looking for someone?"

"Nah, just checking out the women. You know me, always have my ride home lined up early in the evening."

Spence laughs. "Yeah, whatever, mate. I don't think she's coming tonight."

"Who are you talking about?" I take a big sip of my drink.

"You know who I'm talking about. Your charm last night couldn't have worked."

"Fuck off." I finish my drink and push the glass towards him. "Fill it up."

He takes my glass and laughs. When he has poured me another one, he gives it back to me. "I heard you talking to her when you were at the bar. You need to learn to whisper. Damn, it was hot though!" He walks off, laughing to himself.

Fuck. That's all I need, Spence thinking I've gone soft.

I walk out to the office and chat to Stig and Jeannie for a while. Still no sign of her. I can't ask them about her; that would be too awkward.

"Nate, aren't you supposed to be getting the music ready for the second half?"

I look at the time. "Fuck. Can't stay here talking. Gotta go."

I have one eye on the door all night. Waiting, hoping, praying she will turn up.

She doesn't. I don't stay for drinks after all the customers have left; I go home on my own instead. I had plenty of offers but none of them compared to her.

She has me tied up in a knot.

Moving On

"Ruby, can I meet you for lunch, or even for a drink after you've finished work? I really need to see you. I have a contract I need you to read over urgently."

"Of course. What about if we go to Miss Q's? They do great food and it will be quiet enough this evening to talk. I'll be finished with work around seven, so do you want to meet me at seven thirty?"

"That's perfect. Thank you, Ruby."

I hang up the phone and smile at Scottie. "That's the first thing sorted, now to find somewhere to live. Are you going to come with me or are you working?"

"Sorry, babe. I'm working today, but I can meet you in Miss Q's as well. I know Ryan is working too, but I think Jose is off today. Give him a ring and I'm sure he will be delighted to meet you and go flat hunting."

"Great idea. I'll send him a text."

I say goodbye to Scottie and Ryan and arrange to meet them later in Miss Q's.

Hey Jose. Are you free today?

I don't wait long for his reply.

Yeah babe xx just tell me where and when xx

He makes me laugh. He is absolutely gorgeous and he knows it. He thinks that every woman, including me, wants to sleep with him. I don't and he hates it.

Great, meet me at The Slug & Lettuce near Covent Garden in two hours.

See you then sweet cheeks xx

I laugh to myself. Sweet cheeks–who says that?

From Scottie's spare room, I transform into Pinkie, but this time it's daytime Pinkie that makes an appearance. When I think I'm acceptable, I leave Scottie's and make my way to Covent Garden on the Underground. I'm starting to enjoy the Underground. There are so many interesting people and no one stares at my bright pink hair.

I take the District line to South Kensington and

then change onto the Piccadilly line to Covent Garden. It takes me about twenty-five minutes. I love the feeling of climbing out from underneath the city, and then the feeling of the fresh air when it hits my face when I reach ground level.

I turn around a few times, looking around me. It is definitely different trying to navigate around the city on foot rather than letting Tony drive me.

I walk into the Slug & Lettuce and Jose is at the bar. He turns to look for me and smiles when he sees me. "Hey, sweet cheeks. Grab a table. I've got you a drink."

I nod and find a table by the window. He's a friend and I know he understands our relationship, but I still don't trust him enough to sit at the back of the pub with him.

He raises his eyebrows at me when he sees the table I got us by the window.

"See you still don't trust yourself around me," he says as he puts our drinks down and kisses me on the cheek.

I laugh. "No, I don't."

"How're things, Pinkie?" he asks as he takes a gulp of his drink.

"They are absolutely appalling, to be honest. Things at home have spun out of control. So much so that I need to go apartment hunting today. That's why I wanted you to come with me and help me pick."

He claps his hands. "Oh, yeah. I love looking at how everyone else lives."

If I didn't know better, I would think Jose is gay. He looks like he is, he acts like he is, but I've been told that he is one hundred percent red-blooded male.

We talk about where I want to live. Covent Garden is very vibrant during the day and comes alive at night, but Soho is the up and coming area to live in.

"Come on. Let's go and have a look at a couple of places here and then head over to Soho to see a few. We should have a better idea later and then I can make a decision after I've had time to think about it."

We both down our drinks and leave to find the local letting agency. By five o'clock, I'm wrecked. We've seen two properties in Covent Garden, and as much as I want to live there, I didn't like them. They were very nice, open planned, huge, floor to ceiling windows and a gorgeous view, but they didn't scream 'home' to me.

Jose is getting pissed off. "Can we get another drink before we go and look at this last one, please?"

"Okay. Just one though. After this one, we're going back to Earl's Court to meet the others. Don't forget I'm going to ring Whiskey Sour and see if I can get you all in tonight, so stop moaning. It's no wonder you're single." I laugh.

He pushes me on the arm.

We saw one property in Soho, and although it was nice, I'm still not sure. I like the look of this property though, and it isn't too far from Whiskey Sour. If I don't get the job Whiskey offered me, there are plenty of other places I can work close by.

Jose takes me into The Coach & Horses, which is a pub renowned for its moody and ignorant landlord, but you're always guaranteed a good time where something will kick off. There is so much character here and I love it already. We quickly down our drinks because we want to get into this place, have a look, and then make our way to our friends.

We meet the letting agent and she takes us in the lift and presses for the Penthouse Two. I smile to myself; this is more like it.

When the door opens, it opens directly into a stunning apartment.

"Wow, this is gorgeous," I say, stepping out of the lift.

"You need a key to get the lift to stop here so no one can come up unless you've given them a key or you've told the concierge that you want them to come up. So, security is not an issue."

We start to look around. There's an open plan

kitchen, dining room, and lounge area with a wraparound balcony. We stand out there and look down at the view. We're really close to Piccadilly Circus so noise is an issue, but it's not too bad up here.

"Pinkie, this is amazing. What I would give to live here," Jose says, spinning around.

"Come on. Let's look at the bedrooms," I say, dragging him to the internal lift that takes us upstairs to the second storey of this duplex.

The bedrooms are beautiful. There are three of them in total. Too many for me, but then I have lots of friends who I'm sure would love to stay over.

The master bedroom has a full bathroom en-suite with a huge walk-in shower and a full-size bath. There is a balcony outside two of the bedrooms, connecting them.

Jose grabs my hand and pulls me outside. "Pinkie, seriously. Do you really think you could live here? Do you know how happy it would make me to see you living here? I can stay over all the time. It would be fantastic." He is getting a little carried away with himself and he pulls me close and hugs me.

We break apart and stand looking over the balcony, pointing out landmarks that we know. We laugh and joke and then I look at my watch.

"Shit. Jose, we need to go if we're meeting Ruby and Scottie in half an hour, and we still have to get there. I'll ring Whiskey Sour on my way and see if we can get in tonight."

"Yeah, sweet cheeks. That would just be the topping on this fantastic day. Thank you for letting me come with you. I hope you take this one. It really suits you."

We run inside and slam the door closed. I turn to the letting agent and tell her, "I want it! When can I move in?"

She looks me up and down as if to say that I can't afford this place, but then she swallows her pride. A sale is a sale to her, after all.

"We can do the paperwork now and then we'll contact you tomorrow when we've worked out the financials and references, etc."

"I can do all of that. I have a guarantor too, but you have no worries on the financials, honey. I'm Jennifer Hamilton Wade from Wades of Sloane Street."

She gasps. "No problem, Miss Jennifer. We will have everything sorted and you can collect the keys tomorrow. Does that suit you?"

Now she decides to be nice to me. I guess money does talk.

I complete the paperwork then say, "'Til tomorrow. I can't wait to move in here. This is a private let and I don't want the media knowing about this. Okay?"

"Of course, Miss Jennifer. We're very discreet."

I smile and shake her hand and then we get in the lift. When we get onto the street, I start jumping up and down like Jose did and he soon joins me.

"I'm so excited, Jose. This is the start of a new chapter in my life."

He looks at me. "Are you really Jennifer Hamilton Wade?"

I smile and nod. "Yes, I am."

"Why the pink hair and dress up?"

"I wanted people to like me and not judge me for my money or financial status. I feel liberated when I'm Pinkie. Jennifer makes me feel claustrophobic and my home life is not good at all. Pinkie is my escape. I think I'm more Pinkie than Jennifer right now."

He hugs me tight. "Well, I love Pinkie and I'm so glad we're friends."

"Me too, Jose." He tries to kiss me. "But not that good friends." I laugh and pull away.

"Damn. It was worth trying!" He starts to laugh as well and the two of us run down to the Underground and make our way over to Earl's Court.

When I woke up this morning, I never expected to see Pinkie with another man.

When I woke up this morning, I never expected to feel jealous.

When I woke up this morning, I never expected to realise that I actually give a fuck.

I was pissed off last night when I came home on my own. Pinkie was everywhere in my mind. Every time I closed my eyes, she was there, taunting me.

What is it about her that draws me to her? She makes me want things I've never wanted before. I not only want to bring her to my place, but I want her to wake up here in the morning after I've fucked her into submission. I want her to spend lunchtime with me, and then the next night, and the next night.

I walk into my bedroom and take a cold shower. It's not working. I still see her when I close my eyes. I imagine what she looks like under those tight clothes that hug her body. I want to know what she looks like bare. No pink wig. No clothes. No image to hide behind. I want to know the real girl behind Pinkie.

After taking care of my erection in the shower, I realise I'm hard again. God, I need to fuck her brains out. Maybe then I can move on from these confusing feelings.

I hear noises out on the balcony next to mine. I've lived here for five years, and I love it. It's central and I hear the noise of the city, but I'm so high up that I feel like I'm away from it all.

The apartment next door has been up for rent for about three months. It's expensive and no one wants to spend the money in this area. That suits me though, because it means I don't have to worry about noisy neighbours. That looks like it might change soon. I recognise that voice. I'd recognise it anywhere. Pinkie. What the fuck is she doing here?

I open my sliding door and peek outside. She's standing there with a guy. A good-looking guy. What the fuck?

I make sure I'm hidden from her view, but I can hear them talking.

"Pinkie, seriously. Do you really think you could live here? Do you know how happy it would make me to see you living here? I can stay over all the time. It would be fantastic." He grabs her and hugs her.

I growl. Really? I hate seeing him touch her. I want to punch him, but I need to listen to find out who he is to her. As for staying over, that's not going to happen on my watch.

They're leaning over the balcony and they seem to pointing at things and laughing, but all I can do is look at her beautifully luscious arse. My cock gets harder and I want to jump over the balcony and thrust it inside her cheeks. I want to mark her as mine. He needs to get his hands away from her.

Suddenly, she stands up and touches his arm.

"Shit. Jose, we need to go if we're meeting Ruby and Scottie in half an hour and we still have to get there. I'll ring Whiskey Sour on my way and see if we can get in tonight."

"Yeah, sweet cheeks. That would just be the topping on this fantastic day. Thank you for letting me come with you. I hope you take this one. It really suits you," pretty boy says.

Fucking 'sweet cheeks'. Who the fuck says that? Who says that to my woman? No one, that's who. I am absolutely livid; I can barely control myself, and then I remember she said she wants to go to Whiskey Sour tonight. She's going to ring them to see if she can get her friends in.

I smile. I need to ring Stig and tell him to let her and her friends in–it doesn't matter how many. I want them all there. I want them all to know that she's mine, and pretty boy can see it too. He touched her one too many times for my liking.

I stand outside on the balcony and look down. I see him hug her and then he tries to kiss her.

"Fucker, get your hands off her!" I shout down at them. They don't hear me but I notice she pulls away from him and doesn't let him kiss her. She punches him on the arm and then he takes her hand and they run towards the Underground.

I go back into my bedroom and sit on the end of the

bed. She is killing me. She has my fucking balls in the palm of her hand and she doesn't even know it.

I ring Stig. "Hey. It's Nate."

"What's up? Not like you to ring me 'cos you miss me." He laughs loudly.

"Fuck off. I need a favour."

"Shoot. Whatever you want."

"Pinkie is going to ring you to find out how many friends she can bring in tonight on her membership. I want you to tell her that, tonight, she can bring however many she wants. It won't be many, but tell her this is a one-time deal and unless they buy memberships, they will only be able to come one at a time."

"You know that's against the rules, Nate. Sawyer would have my nuts on a plate."

"I know. I'll square it with him. I think she might be thinking about taking the job Whiskey offered her, so please give her an exception tonight."

"If I get my balls hauled over the coals, it's your fault, and you will owe me big time."

"I know. Thanks, mate. See you later."

Seven

Introduction To Whiskey Sour

We've had a lovely dinner in Miss Q's and now we're sitting in a booth at the back of the pub. I've taken out the agreement that my lovely parents gave me.

"Fuck, Pinkie. This sucks majorly," Ruby says in between sips of her drink. She's been looking at the contract for the last twenty minutes. We've all watched her, and every now and then she makes an exasperated sound and flicks the page over.

"Can you help me with it? Is there a way out of it?"

She starts to shake her head. "Not that I can see straight away, but we've got six months to find a loophole, haven't we?"

"Yeah, we do. I was so angry that I just signed it without reading it. I didn't think there was another way out. I know that was stupid and I wish I'd taken the time to read it first."

"Do you want to tell us all about it?" Scottie says.

"Well, you know the story and I'm guessing Ruby does now she's read the contract, but basically, my parents are going to make me marry someone they choose for me. They found out about Pinkie and told me I have six months to get Pinkie out of my system and do whatever I have to do and then marry their choice at the end of it. They told me if I didn't sign it then they would disown me and cut me off. So, by signing it, I have effectively given myself six months to get Pinkie out of my system. Maybe after six months I'll be ready to go home and marry who they want me to marry. It could be just an act of rebellion before I have to settle down. It's not like I'm going to fall in love in six months, is it?

They might pick someone for me to marry that I actually like. That wouldn't be too bad, would it?" I look at them all with pity in their eyes. I know they think I'm trying to talk myself into it.

"What happens if they pick someone awful?" Jose asks.

"If I don't marry their choice at the end of the six months then they will sue me for everything I spend during that time."

"Nice parents!"

"I know, right? Living the dream. What I want to do is try and get out of the contract at the end of the six months and not have to pay them back any money. They're my parents. They should love me and want me to be happy. Right?"

"Yeah, they should, but we know they aren't like most parents. I'll do everything I can to find a loophole or something to get you out of this contract. I can't promise anything though," Ruby says, reaching across and putting her hand on top of mine.

"I know." I smile at her.

Jose says, "So, is that why you were looking at apartments today? Don't you think you should have lowered your prices a bit if you have to pay for it yourself?"

"I suppose I should have, but a part of me wants them to pay for it and then I'm going to fight it to the bitter end. I'm going to get a job and start saving my own money. That way, in six months, I can live off my own means if I don't go home."

"But... that apartment is three thousand pounds a month!"

Everyone gasps.

"I know. They can afford it, believe me. I'm used to staying in luxury wherever I go, so why should I change that now? I know if I don't marry their choice at the end of the six months then I won't be living a life of luxury, so I'm going to enjoy it while I still can."

"Hear, hear," Scottie says, holding his glass up to

clink against mine. We all clink glasses and then take a sip.

Scottie looks at me. "So... did you ring Whiskey Sour?" He's like a little boy going into a sweet shop for the first time.

I laugh. "Yes, I did. Stig, that's the guy in the membership office, said that for one night only I can bring all of you guys, but after that, the membership is only for me and one of my friends. If you all want to come again then you can come on your own memberships."

"Yeah, like that's going to happen," Ryan says.

I wink at him. "Ryan, you never know what's going to happen in the next six months."

Ruby looks down at her work clothes.

"Erm, I cannot go to a club like this. Can we go home and then meet later? I need to be sexy to go to a club like that."

I think about Nate and how I want to look sexy for him. "Yeah, that's a good idea." I say, thinking about what I can wear.

We all leave and agree to meet again at ten o'clock at Scottie's house. When we get back there, I take a bath, then I stand in front of my suitcase and try to work out what I can wear that will make him want me. Although, so far, it didn't matter what I wore. He just took what he wanted.

A buzz rushes over me. I lie on the bed and think about Nate; his long hair, his tattoos, and his chiselled face with his dimple. He is absolutely gorgeous and I want him.

I run my hands gently over my body. My nipples start to harden as I think of him taking them in his mouth; I don't think he would be gentle. I think he would bite down on them. I pinch them to try and simulate the same feeling. I arch my back off the bed. God, that went straight down to my clit.

My hand trails down my flat stomach and then disappears between my legs. I'm wet just thinking of him. I plunge a finger inside. It's hot, wet, and it turns me on. I groan. God, this man is driving me mad and he's not even in the room.

All of a sudden, I hear a knock on the door.

"You better not be making a mess on my sheets in there, Pinkie," Scottie says, laughing.

"Fuck you!"

"No, thanks!" He laughs and I hear him walking down the corridor to his bedroom.

The moment has gone and now I'm frustrated. I hope, tonight, Nate is going to satisfy me.

I put on a black dress which is figure hugging and short. I don't wear any knickers because they would be visible through the dress. I've shaved and I'm bare between my legs. Sensations are heightened by having no hair and I know I have to be careful what I sit on because it could really turn me on.

I put on my over the knee boots and my short black leather jacket. I look in the mirror. Perfect Pinkie style.

Ruby and Jose arrive together and then we're ready to go. We have a few shots before the taxi arrives.

When we pull up to the door of Whiskey Sour, I pay for the taxi and then knock at the door.

Scottie is beside himself. I can feel the excitement from all my friends and realise that was how I was the other night when Drew brought me here. Was it really only a couple of nights ago? Drew seems like someone who is way in my past.

Stig opens the door. "Hey, Pinkie. How are you and all your friends?"

I smile at him. "We're good, and thank you so much for organizing that we can all come in."

"No worries at all."

"I'd like to see Whiskey later, if that's okay?"

"I'll tell her you were looking for her. Now, you all go and have a great time."

The first thing I do is look for Nate; I can't see him.

Everyone goes to the bar and Spence notices me.

"Hey, Pinkie! How's tricks? Thought you would have been in last night."

I wonder why he thought that. "No. I had some personal shit I had to deal with last night."

"Okay, I see. What can I get you all?" They all tell him what they want to drink and I turn to look at the dance floor. The show hasn't started yet so there are customers dancing and the music is making me sway my hips too.

I pay for the drinks and then, after we find a table, Ruby and I head to the dance floor.

I'm still looking for Nate, but he isn't in his booth. The music must be pre-set tonight. I wonder if he will be here at all.

I move to the music. It's sensual, sexual, and I'm so turned on. I open my eyes and Ruby says, "Damn, Pinkie. I love cock, but you make me want to be a lesbian right now. You are fucking hot!"

I laugh. "I'm only dancing. Don't be so stupid."

She laughs and we carry on dancing.

The music changes and I feel an electricity in the air that wasn't there before. Nate must be watching me; I can feel him. I move my hips more. I touch myself more. I exaggerate everything more. It's all for him.

Roxette's *She's Got The Look* starts to play.

I laugh to myself. He likes what he see's tonight.

We go back to our table and have another drink,

but we don't sit down; there will be time enough for that.

When we get back on the dance floor *Private Eyes* by Hall & Oates is playing.

I throw my head back and laugh. He has a great sense of humour. He's letting me know he's watching me.

We dance for another two songs, each as poignant as the last. We start to go back to the table when I say, "Ruby, I'll meet you back there. I'm going to the toilet before the show starts."

"Yeah, no problem," she says without looking at me.

My heart is hammering in my chest. I hope he follows me. I need him to follow me.

I walk slowly to the toilet but he doesn't come. I'm disappointed and I sit in the bathroom for a few minutes. I open the door and I don't get assaulted by him; he's not there.

Just as I think he's not interested, just as I'm about to walk back into the club, a hand grabs mine and pulls me down the corridor then pushes me through a door.

"Get off me!" I shout.

"No!" I look up and it's Nate. "Here with your new boyfriend, are you? Drew can't even be home and here you are flaunting another guy in front of my face. Are you trying to make me jealous? Is that it?"

"What are you talking about? Those are my friends and you can't tell me who I can go out with."

He pushes me against the wall. "Really? I can't?" He leans against me and kisses me. He smashes his lips to mine and grinds down on them.

Holy hell, that's hot. This man turns me on just looking at him, so having him touch me like that, I can feel myself getting wet. His hand starts to run down my body and under my dress.

He pulls away. "Fuck, Pinkie. You don't have any knickers on."

I laugh. "No. I don't. I wanted to be ready tonight, just in case you accosted me."

He leans his forehead against mine. "Accosted? You think that's what I'm doing?" He laughs.

His hand hasn't left my thigh and it starts to move closer and closer to my core.

"I want you so much. You drive me insane."

I reach down and run my hand along the outline of his cock. "I want you too. What are you going to do about it?"

He growls at me then lifts me up and places me on a work bench. I don't even know where I am, or what type of room this is. I don't care. All I care about is this man in front of me.

He positions me so I'm barely on the counter; my legs are spread and he is in between them. I hear the zipper on his jeans open. He takes his cock out and I look at it. Oh. My. God. It's huge. I get wetter just thinking about it inside me.

I wriggle further to the edge, hoping he will fuck me here and now. He slaps his cock on my clit.

"Oh God, Nate. Give me your cock. I need it. Now!"

He groans as he thrusts inside me. He's huge. It hurts. "Oh, God. Oh, God."

He chuckles. "No, duchess. It's all me." He stills to let me get used to his size but he doesn't wait long. He starts pounding my pussy with everything he's got. He is certainly giving me a good fucking. that's for sure.

I wrap my legs around his waist and pull his arse in closer. I need everything he has. My stilettos are sticking into his arse but he doesn't seem to care.

"Fuck, Pinkie. This feels too good!"

He squeezes my nipple and it sends me over the top.

"Fuck!" I scream as I come all over his cock. He pounds me harder and then, at the last minute, he pulls it out and comes all over my pussy.

All I can hear is our heavy breathing. I don't know what to say to him now.

"That was..."

I wait with bated breath to hear what he has to say.

"You're a good lay, duchess. See you later. Hope

pretty boy measures up for you now." He zips himself up and walks out of the door.

"What the fuck?" I scream. Has he seriously just fucked me and left me here? What the fuck does he mean by *pretty boy*?

I'm disappointed, disheartened, and embarrassed. I thought our attraction was mutual, that he wanted me as much as he said he did. I just made a right tit of myself.

I make it to the toilet and clean myself up, and then I hold my head up high and walk back out to my friends.

"Are you okay, Pinkie? You were gone a while and you seem kind of flushed," Ruby asks.

"I'm fine. Look, the show is starting. I'm so excited."

I have never been as happy to see the lights go dark, knowing that Nate can't see me now. A tear runs down my face. Maybe I should just marry the man my parents choose. Maybe there is no 'one true love' out there for me. Maybe I won't have passion in my life. I want it though. I want all of that. I thought Nate might give me that, but I guess I was wrong about that as well.

The show is amazing, but I don't enjoy it as much as I did the other nights. Nate has seen to that. He has taken the light from behind my eyes. I go to the bar as the girls are about to start their freestyle section. Nate has to do the music so I know he won't be watching me.

"Hey, Spence. Can you get me a shot of something strong and hard, please?"

"That kind of a night, is it?"

"You could say that. Listen, I was hoping to see Whiskey. Is she around?"

"Yeah, she's in the office. I'll take you." He comes around my side of the bar and then he takes me across the front of the stage which is thankfully in darkness and then brings me down the corridor to a room that says *Security* on it.

He laughs. "I'll just check she's there. Sometimes there's things going on in there that you don't want to see, believe me. I've walked in on them more times than I care to remember." He very cautiously opens the door and then smiles.

"It's safe. They're both dressed." He opens the door for me to go inside.

"Thanks, Spence," I say, and he closes the door.

"How can I help you?" Whiskey asks.

"I was wondering if your offer of a job still stands." I wring my hands together. I've never had to ask someone for a job and I've never depended on anyone saying yes as much as I need her to right now.

"I saw you out there again tonight. Damn, you know how to dance. I saw a few of the men rubbing their cocks. I thought it might have been a one off thing with you, but, no. They all want you so badly. I'd be foolish to turn you down." She stands up and shakes my hand.

"Welcome to the sweet girls of Whiskey Sour!"

"Seriously? Oh, thank you so much." I reach out and hug her. This is too momentous for handshakes.

I hear Sawyer laughing behind her. "You did good, girl."

"Stay after for a drink with the girls and then we can talk about what happens next."

"Okay. I'm with friends though."

"They can stay too, and if we're late, we'll make sure you get home."

"Thanks. You don't know how much this means to me." I have tears in my eyes.

"I probably do. Whiskey Sour was my salvation, and one day, I might tell you my story. I know you have a story within you too. You might get us to help you one day when you can trust us enough to tell us."

She hugs me again and then slowly turns me towards the door and pushes me out. "Get out and let me celebrate this great news with my husband."

I laugh.

As the door closes, I hear her say, "Fuck, Sawyer. Did you have to get your cock out when she was still in here?"

I chuckle and hear him say, "Get on it and shut the fuck up. Come here, beautiful."

Wow. Just wow.

I'm so excited, I don't see Nate leaning against the door. "What the fuck do you want? Move!"

I reach out to grab his arm to move him out of my way, but he doesn't budge. "What's the problem, duchess? Worried pretty boy isn't going to measure up?"

"Fuck you. I thought you were different. How fucking wrong was I? You're just like I thought you would be. A fucking douchebag."

He stands there gawping at me and then very slowly moves out of my way, but as I walk past him, he grabs my arm. He pulls me so his mouth is near my ear. "This is not over. You'll be back to me when pretty boy isn't enough for you."

"I don't know what the fuck you're talking about. Now, let me get past."

He moves and lets me walk back to my table.

"Hey, guys. Guess what?"

"What?" Jose says, jumping up and down in his seat.

"You are now looking at the latest member of the sweet girls of Whiskey Sour."

"No freaking way!" Ruby says, hugging me. Jose joins her then Scottie and Ryan join in too.

Jose goes to the bar and orders a round of shots for all of us.

When he comes back with the drinks, we down our shots, making a lot of noise in the process. Everyone turns to look at us but we don't care. We sit down to watch the finale and, boy, was it good. There were some pyrotechnics thrown in there too.

After the lights come back on, we stay, talking. I can see Scottie and Ryan are ready to go home.

"Why don't you guys go? I have to stay longer to see the girls and work out schedules. Whiskey said she would make sure I get home. I have your key, Scottie."

"Do you mind? All this gyrating has made me horny," Scottie says, giving Ryan his best come-to-bed eyes.

I laugh. "At least get your fucking and those horrible noises one of you makes out of the way before I get home."

Scottie looks at Ryan and laughs. "I told you she could hear you."

"Fuck. That turns me on even more," Ryan says, grabbing Scottie's hand.

I walk with them out to the front door. Stig calls them a taxi and I wait with them until it arrives.

"I hear you got the job," Stig says.

"Yeah. I'm so excited. I can't wait to start. I'm

hanging around 'til everyone finishes. Will I see you in the bar?"

"You sure will," Stig says as he goes to open the door.

He hasn't even got his hand on the door when it swings open and hits the wall.

"What the fuck?" Stig says, grabbing the person who came through the door.

"Get off me!" It's Nate. "Where the fuck is...?" he says, looking around him wildly. His eyes land on mine and he takes a deep breath.

"What's your problem, Nate? Pinkie is celebrating her new job at Whiskey Sour." He looks at Nate strangely.

Nate visibly relaxes and then he opens the door and says, "After you, duchess."

I flick him the finger and walk through the door. He doesn't follow me. I don't care. He burnt his bridges with me earlier.

We sit around and wait for the show to finish and for everyone to leave. I can see Ruby and Jose are getting tired, but I know what it's like being here. It's like a drug and you don't want to leave.

All the girls come out and sit at our table, then Whiskey, Sawyer, Stig, Jeannie, and finally Nate. Spence brings over his signature drinks and gives me a raspberry Cosmopolitan.

Nate doesn't say anything, which is strange for a man who always has so much to say. He looks like he's grinding his teeth.

Jose touches my arm and I lean closer to him so he can whisper in my ear. "That guy is staring at you like you're his next meal. What's his deal?"

I look over to Nate and laugh. "Don't mind him. He thinks he's God's gift."

"Well, he kind of looks it. Be careful."

"You don't know the half of it."

Nate is staring at me; he doesn't even blink.

Jose sits back up and then leans towards Ruby. She smiles and blushes. She says something back to him and then he reaches his hand down and I'm sure he just adjusted himself. Why didn't I think of them as a couple before? They are so well-suited.

I hear a bang, and when I look up, Nate has slammed his drink down on the table. Everybody is looking at him.

"What's the matter, pretty boy? One woman not enough for you?" he says, staring at Jose.

Wait, did he just call Jose 'pretty boy'? Oh my God. He thinks Jose and I are together. I start to chuckle. I try to keep it under control. I think I'm being quiet, but it gets louder.

Nate turns to look at me. He is staring at me as if he could kill me. "What the fuck are you laughing at?"

Jose doesn't want to hang around. He stands and says, "I'm going home. Come on, babe. We don't need to listen to this shit!"

"Babe?" Nate says, standing up and pushing his chair away from him. "I think you and I need to have a conversation. Outside." He starts to walk towards the front door. He holds the door open for Jose to walk through, but I beat him to it.

"What the fuck is your problem?" I push his chest after the door closes behind us all. "First of all you attack me in the corridor... twice. Then you fuck me in a cupboard. Now I think you're accusing me of sleeping with one of my best friends. Really, Nate?"

"I saw you two today. You were hugging and he was saying things..."

"So? What business is it of yours?" I'm right up in his face.

He looks past me to Ruby and Jose who are kissing, and I'm sure Jose is grinding against her.

I turn back to him. "See? Not cool!" I turn to leave.

He grabs my arm. "I'm sorry." Those are two words I never expected to hear come out of his mouth.

"I'm confused. The other night when I was with Drew, you told me you wanted me. Tonight, you took me and then you didn't want me. So, if it's a one night fuck, then fine, but don't start accusing me of things. You have no right to do that. It's not like..."

I don't get to finish what I'm saying because he slams me against the wall and kisses me. Not gently and lovingly, but rough and hard. I love it.

"I told you I wanted you. I told you to be here last night when Drew had gone home. You didn't come. Then I saw you in town with *him*, hugging and talking about him staying over at your place and I just saw red. I thought you were playing me."

"Something happened last night and I couldn't come. I needed to be with my friends. But why just fuck me and then turn on me, Nate? That hurt like a bitch."

"I'm sorry." He kisses my neck and all the way up to my ear. "I'm really sorry, duchess. I didn't want to be the other guy. The guy you fuck when you feel like it. I want more with you." He shakes his head like he can't believe what he's saying.

Jose reaches out to touch my arm, but Nate pulls it away. "Don't you touch her!" he says, pulling me closer still.

Jose laughs at him. "Whatever, mate. Good luck taming her." I make a face at him and he sticks his tongue out at me. "Our taxi is here, and since you've been talking about fucking, I have a raging hard on and I'm taking Miss Ruby home to fuck her senseless, so excuse me if I don't want to be a part of your game anymore."

He walks past us, and as he walks out the door, he says, "Pinkie, you need me, just shout!" Then he's gone.

I look at Nate then double over with laughter.

"What is the matter with you?" he says, trying to make me stand up.

"You. Everything you just said is so not what I would associate with you. You are the biggest player to walk this planet and I'm not about to be played. There is too much at stake in my life."

He takes me and lifts me up. I automatically wrap my legs around his waist. "I can assure you I'm not playing you. I want you. I need you. I will have you." He crashes his lips to mine and kisses me into submission.

When we part, I say, "I need to go back and talk to Whiskey about my job. Are you going to behave?" I chuckle.

"If I have to." He takes my hand, pulling me behind him into the club.

I sit next to Pinkie at the table and everyone is looking at me. Sawyer keeps laughing and shaking his head. Stig just keeps staring at me and then whispering to Jeannie. They are all doing my fucking head in.

I put my hand on her leg. I need to touch her, to know she's there. She ignores it; she's talking to Whiskey.

"The way it works, Pinkie, is that you have to come in to see Beau. He's the dance teacher. He will watch you dance and decide what type of dancing suits you. He will talk to Nate about the type of music that works best for you." She looks at me. "Although, from the type of music he has been playing these last few nights, he has obviously worked that out for himself." Everyone around the table chuckles. "Beau will then work out the finale with a new troupe member and when he's happy that it's going to work, you can join the troupe."

"Perfect. I was worried about having to go out on stage alone, so I love the sound of that. When is the next dance class?" Pinkie asks.

Jeannie smiles. "Tomorrow at four. I might be leaving the troupe so you can take my place."

There are cries of, "No way. Why?"

"I just want to spend more time with Stig and..." she rubs her stomach. "... baby Stig is on the way now too."

Everyone congratulates them and I think I see Stig blush.

Whiskey whispers to Spence and then he comes out with a couple of bottles of champagne and lots of glasses. He also brings out a cocktail for Jeannie. "This is a virgin Bloody Mary." He winks at her. She smiles.

We stay talking until about five in the morning. Then, one by one, everyone starts to leave. Pinkie turns to me. "I need to order a taxi so I can go home. I'm sure Scottie and Ryan have finished and gone to sleep by now."

"I'll order you a taxi, but you're coming home with me."

"No. I need to go home. It's been a long and draining night." She stands up and starts to turn to leave. I grab her waist and pull her back into my chest. I place one hand at the base of her stomach and the other one across her shoulders. I pull her back, kiss her neck, and suck her earlobe.

"I don't care if you're tired. You are coming home with me. I want you in my bed, duchess. I want to fuck you until you don't even know your own name."

I feel her squeeze her legs together; she is as affected as I am.

"Come on, duchess. I need you to myself."

I say goodbye to everyone and then we walk out to wait for a taxi. When we get into the back, she lies on me and starts to fall asleep.

I watch her. She is gorgeous and I'm so happy I found her. When we get out at my apartment, she doesn't even realise that I live next door to the apartment she wants to rent.

I carry her from the lift to my bed and slowly undress her. She barely wakes. So, I do something I have never done before. I lay her on the bed, remove my clothes, and climb in naked behind her. I pull her back so I'm surrounding every part of her and wrap my arm around her. Once I know she's safely in my arms, I kiss her shoulder and then fall asleep. It feels like heaven.

Eight

I can't move. Something is holding onto me, making me feel hot. Where the hell am I and who the hell is behind me?

I slowly turn around and see Nate, fast asleep. As I move, he pulls me back to him and holds me tight. "Mine!" he says. I giggle.

I try to move again and he does the same.

This is hilarious. Then he pulls me closer.

"Where do you think you're going, duchess?"

"I... I... thought you were asleep."

"I was until you started to move and rubbed against my cock. Now he's awake, so I have to be awake." He growls.

"Well, I'm terribly sorry I woke him. God, you're grumpy this morning."

"I'm not grumpy. I'm just trying to control myself."

I laugh again. "Why? You haven't been able to so far. Why is it different today?"

"Because, today, I want to show you that it's more than fucking." He pushes me down onto my back and leans over me. "You have made me want more. I like you a lot. You challenge me, you annoy me, you amuse me and I want to fuck you most of the time. It scares the crap out of me, but then I look at you and I know that I want to know you, want to laugh with you, want to spend time with you, and that fucking frightens me even more.

"I bet you say that to all the women you bring back here," I say, smiling up at him.

His face clouds over. "I've never brought a woman up here. Ever."

"Really?"

"Yeah. You're the first, and if I have my way, the last."

I smile at him. He knows all the right things to say. I lean up and kiss him quickly on the lips. He smiles.

"I think we can do better than that," he says as he leans down and devours my mouth.

When he kisses me, it sends vibrations all the way down to my core. As he's leaning above me, I can feel his huge cock pushing against me and I know that I want him inside me. I open my legs.

He stops kissing me. "I want to take my time with you this morning."

"Fuck that. I need you inside me now, Nate. Can we go slow next time?"

He laughs so hard his cock feels like it's tickling me. "Anything you say, duchess." He pushes himself in with no foreplay or anything. I'm wet enough for him and he fills me up.

"Oh, that feels so good." I buck my hips to take him fully inside.

"Duchess, do that again, please."

I do, but this time he catches my hips and lifts them off the bed. He wraps my legs around his neck as he pounds into me. It's so deep I think he's going to come out of my mouth.

"You feel so good. We fit each other perfectly." He pounds in harder and faster then reaches down and starts rubbing my clit. That's it for me. It sends me spiralling down.

"Oh, duchess. I can't hold on much longer."

"Then... don't," I say in between breaths.

He pounds harder four more times and then he holds still. His face is scrunched up and his eyes are tightly closed. He looks like a baby and it makes him even more adorable.

We lay there wrapped in each other, not talking. He holds me tight. He kisses the top of my head and this means more to me than any of the other kisses.

"I need to go, Nate. I have somewhere to be."

"Where do you have to be that is better than right here in my bed?"

"I'm moving into my new apartment today."

He chuckles.

"What's funny about that?"

"Nothing, duchess. Come here. You can wait a little bit longer. It won't take you long to get there."

"How do you know? God, you're annoying sometimes. You just have to boss me around. don't you?"

He starts laughing. "Get over here and kiss me." He reaches out to grab me, but I climb off the bed. He follows me and stalks me until I'm backed up against his bedroom window.

He stands in front of me and turns me around. He wraps his arms around me and then opens the door to the balcony. He pushes me outside and we stand looking at the view for a few minutes. "Where is it, duchess? Which direction?"

I look around. It all looks familiar but everything looks different up here. He points his arm over the balcony. "That's Piccadilly Circus down there."

"What?" I turn slowly and look at the apartment next door to his. It dawns on me that we're next door to the apartment that I'm going to rent. "No way!" I turn to look at him and start laughing. "Am I going to be your new neighbour?"

He laughs and holds out his hand to shake mine. "You sure are, duchess. Welcome to the neighbourhood."

I can't believe it. This could get awkward.

"The only way for me to get to your apartment is to go back downstairs in the lift and then back up in yours. Unless, of course, I climb across the balcony."

Shit. I need to think about this. What we have is fun and temporary. It could get really awkward when we stop fucking but are still working together.

"Stop overthinking it, duchess. I'd rather you move in with me than a new apartment but I know you won't do that. Yet."

"Of course I won't. I've only known you for a few days and who knows if we will do this..." I point between me and him, "... again!"

He growls at me and pins me into the corner of the balcony then lowers his mouth onto mine. "You're mine. Of course we will be doing it again. I told you, next time, I'm going to go slower and make sure you enjoy every fucking second of it," he says in between kisses.

God, he turns me on so much.

"Nate, I really need to go and see the lady from the letting agency. We can do this later." I pull out of his grasp.

"I'm coming with you," he says, leaving no room for

argument. "Maybe we can christen your new bed, or bathroom, or..."

"I get the picture," I say, laughing at him.

We go back inside to get dressed, but it occurs to me that he will hear my real name when I sign the documents. I don't want my Jennifer life and my Pinkie life to cross over. I know I've told my other friends, but they needed to know to help me out. Shit.

In the lift, I lean into him. "When I have to sign the documents, will you look around to make sure everything is okay and I'm not missing something? I'd appreciate a man's perspective."

"Of course, duchess." He smiles. He must like that I asked him for help.

The handover went really smoothly and Nate didn't find out my real name. He pointed out a few things that the letting agent says she will get sorted immediately. She hands me the key and I'm really excited. She leaves and I feel him coming up behind me. He grabs me by the waist and swings me around. "Welcome, neighbour."

I laugh and he lets me slowly slide down his body. I feel his erection hitting my arse and all the way down my back. When I land on the floor, I turn around and reach up and kiss him. God, he does things to me that I didn't know could happen. He makes me so happy. I know I haven't known him long, but this moment is just perfect.

He pulls away and rests his forehead on mine. "Come on. We need to get your stuff and start moving you in. I'll drive."

I can't bring myself to look at him. "I don't have a lot. It's okay. I'll bring it over later."

He puts his finger under my chin and pulls my face up so he can see my eyes. "I'm helping you move in, duchess. Let's go!"

God, he is insufferable, but secretly, I like him being bossy.

When we get into the lift, he presses the UG button and takes us down into the car park. He takes my hand and guides me over to an Audi SQ5.

"Wow, this is impressive. Whiskey must pay you a lot of money." I run my fingers over the car. It's a metallic navy blue, sleek, and very expensive.

"Yeah, something like that. This is my baby. Well, she was until you came along."

I laugh at him; he is such a softie.

"Right. Where are we going?"

"Earl's Court, and I'll tell you when we get closer."

We're quiet as he negotiates his way out of the car park and onto the busy streets of London.

"Do you use your car much, Nate?" I ask, turning in my seat to look at him.

"Not really. With Whiskey Sour only being a few streets up, I don't bother. Occasionally, I will take her out for a spin to give her a run. I love the countryside and know that one day I will move out of London, away from all the hustle and bustle. What about you? Where do you like to live?"

I squirm in my seat. "I love the countryside too. The city is too busy for me. I like the peace, quiet, and isolation from London. I've only been with Scottie for a couple of nights, but already it gives me a headache."

"So why move further into the city then?"

"It will be closer to Whiskey Sour and easier for me to get home after work. I don't want to have to spend a fortune in taxis."

"Why would you be bothered about paying for taxis when you're about to move into an apartment that costs more a week than most people get paid in a month?"

"It's a long and complicated story. It's only temporary, anyway. I won't be here longer than six months."

He slams his brakes on and turns to look at me. "What the fuck do you mean?" His face is contorted. His eyes have gone dark and he's looming over me.

"I don't plan to be here longer. Who knows?

Things might change. I... I... have to go back home then."

"Why?" He turns back to look out of the front window; there are cars beeping their horns at him. He doesn't give a shit. He pulls back into the traffic at his own leisure.

"It's a family issue. I'd rather not talk about it, if you don't mind. If things work out between us then I'll tell you. I don't want to expose everything about myself if I don't have to."

"What do you mean? I know we've only known each other a short time, but I'm telling you here and now that you better get used to me being around. I ain't going anywhere. I don't commit to anyone, Pinkie, but I want you in my life. It scares me, but it also feels like the right thing to do."

My heart is flip flopping all over the place. This is what I want in my life. Someone who wants me with passion. Someone who makes me feel whole.

"I want that too, Nate. It's just..." What do I say? I look out the window and see we're in Earl's Court. I start to give him directions, leaving my statement unsaid.

I let us into Scottie's and find it's empty. They're obviously at work. I take him into my bedroom and hurry to put all my stuff together. He watches me the whole time. His brows are furrowed and he's staring at me with frustration.

"I'll take this down to the car. You can pack the rest of your stuff up and then I'll bring it down. If we need to do two trips then we can come back again tomorrow." He turns to walk out of the door and I hear him going out the front door.

I sit on the edge of the bed. I don't have anything else. I only brought one suitcase with me when I left home. Did I do the right thing? I shake my head. Yes, I certainly did. I don't need my parents fixing me up. I can do that myself.

When I go to stand up, I see him standing in the doorway. One arm is grabbing the top of the doorway, and the other is in his pocket. I walk over to him and kiss him. I can't get enough of him.

"Where's the rest of your stuff, duchess?"

I look up and into his eyes. "That's all I have."

His eyes widen. "One day you might trust me enough to tell me what you're running away from and who you really are."

I lean my head onto his chest. He can see straight through me.

"One day, I will." He hugs me and places a gentle kiss on my head.

"Come on then. You have a new job to go to and I have some music to find. We can drop this suitcase off on the way there. I'm excited to see what Beau can come up with for you."

"Me too. What's he like?"

"He's bouncy, flowery, and a pain in the arse. You'll get on with him seeing as you like pretty boys," he says with a smirk.

I punch his arm. "Yeah, I haven't forgiven you for that yet." I shake my head. "Pretty boy," I mutter to myself.

He reaches over and puts his hand on my thigh. He squeezes it and it sends vibrations all the way to the top. "Let's argue about it so we can have lots of fantastic make up sex." He winks at me.

I shake my head at him and laugh.

I'm wrecked. Officially unfit. Beau has broken me.

"Hey, sweetie. You need to keep going. Keep pushing yourself. You need to go to the gym every day," Beau says, smiling at me.

"You like breaking us, don't you?" I say, leaning over and resting my hands on my knees.

"Yes, sweetie. I certainly do." He comes closer to me. "You did really well today. I know you're going to be a great success. You're not my type, but even I wanted to fuck you earlier." He laughs.

"Don't even think about it!" I hear Nate's booming voice. "She's mine. Keep your girly hands off her." He's getting nearer.

"Nate, sweetie. If you're jealous, I'll do you as well. A lovely ménage would be interesting," Beau says, running off in the other direction.

I laugh. "He got you back there."

"I suppose he did, but I didn't like him talking about you like that." He grabs me and pulls me in close to him.

"Nate, listen. We're going to be working together and there will be inappropriate things said. You can't keep chasing people down. Whiskey won't be amused."

"I know, but I don't want anyone touching you. Does that make me a bad person?"

I rest my head on his chest. "No." He is a real softie, but one thing I know is that he really wants me.

"Let's go back to my place," I say. "I have so much unpacking to do and you have work to do tonight. I can unpack when you work."

"No fucking way. You're coming with me."

"I can't come with you to work every night. You need to leave me at home to get settled in."

"Listen, this is the way it's going to go. I want you with me all the time. You won't move in with me so you can come to work with me. It will be a great way to get to know the girls better and be comfortable working at Whiskey Sour. I will stay at yours tonight and you can unpack tomorrow. How does that sound?"

What's the point in fighting him? I love the sound of all of that. "Sounds like a plan." I kiss him and we go back to mine.

I don't know what's wrong with me. I don't want to let her out of my sight. Not because I don't trust her, but because I want to be able to see her or touch her when I want. I feel whole when she's next to me. I have never felt like this about a woman before. I fuck them and roll over onto the next one.

When Pinkie is near me, I feel warm and fuzzy, and when she isn't, I feel cold and dead. I've been through hell to get where I am now and I thought I had everything I ever wanted. Now I know there was always a void in my life, but Pinkie fills that void.

I look out to see if I can find her. From my vantage point in the music booth, I can see almost everywhere. She must be out the back with the girls because I can't see her. I start to panic. I put on a set few songs and then leave the booth to find her.

I go straight out to the changing rooms and barge my way in. The girls are sitting at their tables, looking in their mirrors, making sure that their make-up and hair is beautiful. I've walked in here many times and the girls have been naked and I haven't even looked at them. They don't interest me. Sissy is standing, turned to the side, looking into the mirror at her naked arse. I don't see her though, I'm looking at the woman next to her—Pinkie.

"Hey, duchess. I wondered where you were." I move over to her, kiss her, and pull her in closer to me.

"Nate," she says breathlessly. "Aren't you supposed to be working?"

"Yeah, but I wanted to see you." Sissy starts to giggle. "What are you laughing at, Sissy?"

"You. It's funny to watch you like this. This is not the Nate we know."

I pretend to punch her arm.

Pinkie looks at me and rolls her eyes. "Come on then. Show me how you work the music here." She takes my hand and pulls me out of the changing rooms.

She opens the door to my booth and I kiss her on my way in. "So, this is where the magic happens, huh?"

I laugh. "Yeah. It sure does." I pull up the spare chair for her and show her the deck and all the buttons for the lights and music.

"How come I can never see you when you're in here? You've got a great view."

"The glass is tinted so you can only see out. I don't want everyone watching me when I create magic."

She rolls her chair closer to me. "Really? No one can see anything?"

"Yeah, really," I say, kissing her. I pull back to get started on the music when she stands up then sits on my lap.

"So no one can see me doing this?" she asks as she gyrates on me.

I shake my head.

She reaches down and takes off her top. "Or this ..."

I shake my head again as I reach out and caress one of her tits.

She reaches down and unzips my now throbbing cock. I shake my head.

She stands up and pulls her leggings down to her ankles. I watch her in amazement. Her knickers are next.

When she has kicked them off, she straddles me again and sits on my cock. I slide in fully to the hilt. "Oh, God. You're going to kill me," I say, taking hold of her hips.

"Do you want me to stop?" she asks, trying to get off my lap.

"Don't you fucking dare." I ram her back down again.

"Nate ..."

"I know."

I take her hips and move her up and down with such force I think the chair is going to break.

I kiss her with abandonment. I feel myself fall for her just a little bit more. She challenges me enough to keep me interested and she fits me like a glove.

I can feel her insides starting to quiver and pulsate; I know she's close. I take my finger and run it around her arse, towards her tight hole. I put it in gently, only half an inch or so, but it sends her mad and she orgasms, sucking my cock further into her pussy.

"Fuck, duchess. That was hot," I say to her when we stop panting.

"Yeah, it was. I think I like coming to work with you." She laughs. Then she stands and gets dressed again, looking like nothing happened in here.

Nine

FOUR MONTHS LATER

I smile at Nate as we both check the post boxes. We've just been rehearsing for the new finale we're going to be doing. It's phenomenal and I can't wait to show the world. Nate looks at me. "Mine or yours, duchess?"

"Huh?" I say absentmindedly. I see one of my letters is addressed to Jennifer Hamilton Wade and it looks official. Fuck. How did they find me?

"Are you okay?" he asks, coming up behind me and putting his hand on my waist to pull me in for a hug. I pull away.

"Yeah. Yeah, I'm good. I need to go back to mine. Is that alright? I can come over to yours in half an hour or so."

"What's going on? What's in that letter?" He tries to take it from me, but I don't let him.

"Nate, please. I need to read this letter in private. I promise I won't be long."

"I don't like it. You have to tell me what it is when you come over. If you are any longer than half an hour, I'm jumping that balcony and coming to get you. Do you understand me?"

"Yes, I do." I lean up and kiss him desperately.

"Duchess, what's wrong?" He wraps his arms around me.

"I promise I'll tell you everything today."

"Okay. See you in a bit."

He goes to his lift and I go to mine. Once I'm inside the steel shell, I lean my head back against the mirror. "Fuck!"

I suppose I was hoping they would forget about me. I haven't heard from them in four months so I assumed they would leave me alone and let me live my own life. Looks like I was wrong.

As soon as the door opens, I run into the kitchen and take out the vodka and a glass. I think I need a stiff drink to read this, whatever it is.

I drink one shot, then another, then I look at the beautiful envelope and golden calligraphy writing. I slowly open the envelope, deliberately taking my time.

I take another shot of vodka. I don't care that I have to work tonight. This is a life-changing moment, I can feel it.

I remove the card from the envelope.

Oh my God.

No way.

They can't be serious.

Emily & Leonard

Cordially invite you to

The wedding of their daughter

Jennifer Hamilton Wade

To

Jonathan Elliott Defoe III

On

February fourteenth

At

St Vincent's Church

The card drops from my hand and I sob. The tears are falling off my face. They just broke my heart.

I have a few more swigs of vodka and then my head hits the table and I fall asleep.

"Wake up, duchess. What's wrong? Please wake up. I'm here. I'll help you with whatever you need me to." I hear Nate, but I hear other voices as well.

I start to move. My head hurts.

"Please, duchess. You frightened me," he says, lifting me and wrapping his arm around me. He carries me over to the couch and sits, leaving me across his lap and my head resting on his chest.

"I'm sorry. I'm really sorry."

"Hey, Pinkie. You look like shit, babe." It's Scottie. I smile weakly at him. How did he get here so fast?

I try to move my head to look around, but Nate keeps it firmly against his chest. I look up and see his eyes are dark and concerned. I reach up and put my hand on his chest. "Nate, I'll be okay. I have you."

It takes me another half an hour of just sitting in his lap to be able to talk, but when I sit up and move to the place next to him, I realise it isn't just Nate and Scottie that are here. Ruby, Ryan, and Jose are here too.

"How did you guys get here?" I ask, staring at them.

Nate clears his throat. "When I couldn't wake you, I rang Scottie, panicking. He asked me to read out to him what you had in your hand and when I did, he just said he would be here in fifteen minutes. Then he turned up with all of these people. What's going on?"

I look at Scottie and take his hand to say thank you. "I guess now is the time to tell you what's going on." I look at Ruby and she nods her head.

"Ruby, can you get me out of it? Is there any way at all I can break the contract?"

"What fucking contract are you talking about?"

I need Nate to listen to me and understand what I'm going to say to him.

I take his face in my hands. "You are not going to like what I'm about to say. I have tried everything I can to get out of this. Everything. It looks like they just took my fate into their own hands."

He looks so confused. It's killing me see him like that, but what I am about to say is going to make him worse.

"Go on," he says, not looking me in the eye.

"You see this wedding invite? It's for Jennifer Hamilton Wade. She is rich. Her whole family is rich, but they keep money in the family by marrying off their kids to other families with lots of money."

He nods his head as if he understands but doesn't know why I'm telling him this.

"I'm Jennifer Hamilton Wade."

He looks at me incredulously. He stands up and starts pacing. "Are you fucking kidding me? You're getting married to someone else and you didn't tell me."

I jump up and go after him. "No! You don't understand. They want me to. I don't want to. They are going to make me, Nate."

"They can't force you to walk down the aisle to marry someone you don't know or like. They can't."

"They can! I signed a contract before I left home. I

never thought I would meet someone in the six months that I had before I have to go home. I thought I could spend six months doing what I wanted, try and get out of the contract, and if I couldn't then I would have at least tried. I was going to go back and get married to Jonathan. I never expected to find you though Nate. Never in my wildest dreams.

"So, you're just going to give in and marry this prick?"

I sit down and put my head into my hands.

Ruby stands up and walks over to me. She rests her hand on my shoulder. "Nate, listen to what she's saying. She doesn't want to, she has to. She signed a contract. If she wants to get out of it then she has to pay back everything she's spent since she left."

"I'll pay it back for you. Just don't marry someone else, please." He kneels down so he's at the same height as me. He takes my hands. "I love you. I told you to move in with me. I can look after you. I promise to always look after you."

"I don't know. This card was a shock. I thought they had forgotten about it and would let me get off the hook. How stupid was I? I don't want to marry him. I want to be with you, Nate. I love you too." I start to sob. I can't stop. He lifts me, carries me to the couch again, sits me on his lap, and holds me tight.

"Don't reply to it. We will sort it out. We have

another two months to do something about it. Stay with me. Leave this place. Let me look after you." He tips my chin so that I look up at him and then he leans down and kisses me with so much passion that it makes me cry even more.

When we pull apart, I remember the others are here. "I'm sorry, guys. I don't know what to do."

"I'm going to ring Whiskey and tell her you're not working tonight. You need to rest," Nate says.

"No, please don't. I need to see the girls. I need to dance. I don't want to stay at home on my own."

"You would never be on your own, babe," Scottie says.

"Thank you."

"I wasn't going to leave you, duchess. I'm going to stay with you."

"No. Let's go to Whiskey Sour. I'll talk to the girls and I'll feel better. I know we will work something out."

"I'm going to talk to Spence and Sawyer. They might be able to help us. They're great at helping people in trouble."

I love the way he says 'us' as it means he's not giving up on me.

"I'll go over the contract again and take it into work to see if someone can help us," Ruby says, reaching out for my hand.

"Thanks, babe."

"Right, we need to get ready for work now if you insist on coming in. Do you guys want to come tonight? I'll arrange for passes on the door for you all," Nate says. He really likes my friends, which is fantastic because they're always hanging around my place.

"Hell yeah," Jose says.

Nate smiles. "I'll organise that and we'll see you later. Now we need some time on our own to try and sort out this problem."

After they leave, we lie on my bed and I tell him all about my parents and how awful they've been to me, how they don't really love me, and how they've been making me meet guys they want me to marry who will bring more money into the family. I tell him how Pinkie came about, and then about meeting Scottie and his friends. This leads on to me talking about meeting Drew and how he helped me when I was in a bad place at home.

"I know I said I didn't mind you going home with Drew, but I was lying. I was so jealous because I wanted you so badly," he says as he pulls me closer to him. He kisses me on the head.

"I thought you were, but then I thought you didn't mean any of it, that you were just trying to annoy me."

"No way. I wanted you from the first time I saw you. It was when you were at the front door. I was in the office with Jeannie and I heard this sexy voice and I looked on the camera and I swear my heart skipped a beat when I saw you."

I feel myself blush. "Really?"

"Yeah. Your voice is silky and it caressed me. I knew then I wanted you, and I knew Drew was going back to the States soon so I had to do something quickly or I would miss my chance. I didn't know you were going to buy a membership, but I'm glad I 'accosted' you, as you put it." He kisses me again on the side of my face.

"Me too. They were two of the most exciting moments I had ever experienced. I felt liberated and free. I wanted more of you. You felt like a drug. You still do."

"I'm serious. Move in with me. We can sort everything out together. I promise."

It doesn't matter what he says, I've only got two months left with him, unless a miracle happens. "Yes, I'll move in." I roll over and lay on top of him, kissing him.

"You just made me so happy. I told you I'd not had a woman in my apartment before you. Now there will never be another woman in my apartment, ever!"

He rolls me over so he's top of me and very slowly takes my clothes off, and then takes his own off. He makes love to me very slowly and gently. It makes me cry. He is so gentle and he's trying to tell me how much he loves me.

"Don't cry, duchess."

"These are happy tears, I promise."

We lay holding each other for as long as we can before we have to go to Whiskey Sour.

Pinkie goes to the dressing rooms to get ready with the other girls. I love watching her on stage. She is so sensual, sexual, and I'm sure there are many guys who cream themselves when they see her dance. It's hard to watch others get turned on by her, but she reminds me that it's me who takes her home at night. I still 'accost' her in the hallway whenever I can. I've taken her a few times in the supply cupboard and the things we've done in my music booth I can't even begin to tell you.

I walk over to the bar and ask Spence for a Whiskey Sour. He looks at me. "It's a bit early for the hard stuff, isn't it?"

"Just give it to me. I need a lot of these. I am so fucking annoyed, I want to punch something or someone." I down it in one and slam it back down. "Fill her up and keep them coming."

"Anything I can help you with?"

"I hope you and Sawyer might be able to. Is he around tonight?"

"Yeah, he is. I'll ring him if you want and then we can have a chat later on when we're closed. See if we can help you."

"That would be great. I might go and prime him first though. Stig might want in too. See you after."

I walk out the back to the security office and knock on the door. I always hate just walking in because Sawyer and Whiskey have sex at any time of day or night in any position and don't care who knows it. Sometimes though, it's like catching your mum and dad at it. I chuckle when I hear him telling me to come in.

I open the door cautiously and peek around it. They are both sitting there, smiling. I think I've come in at the end of something. I laugh.

"Sawyer, I need your help with something. Any chance you, me, Spence, and Stig can have a get together after we close tonight? Pinkie is in trouble and we need to help her."

"Is she okay? She's not pregnant is she?" Whiskey says, looking at me with daggers.

I laugh. "If only it were that simple. I'll explain it later and I'm hoping you guys can help me."

"We'll be there to help. See you later," Sawyer says.

I walk out the door and go back to my music booth.

I get a chance to think while I'm in here. I knew Pinkie had a secret because she is very well spoken and I knew she would tell me everything when she was good and ready. I didn't expect it to be this though. I can't lose her. She has come into my life like a steamroller, but I'm not ready to lose her. Not ever.

I set my music up for the night and then I wait to watch her on the stage. The girls are phenomenal tonight. Everyone in the audience is on their feet and clapping after the finale. They're a big hit.

I put on some calming music and then go out to find Pinkie. I need to touch her. I need her close to me.

When I open the door to my booth, she's waiting for me outside. "Thought you would never come out," she says, smiling at me.

"I thought I would never get to hold you again tonight." She touches my chest and then jumps up to put her hands around my neck and her legs around my waist.

"Did I tell you how much I love you?" she asks, snuggling into my neck.

"Not yet, but you can show me later." I kiss her hard and ram her up against the wall.

"What about now? We can go in your booth and lock the door if you want."

"You dirty minx. Tonight, we have bigger fish to fry. We're meeting with the lads to talk about your *wedding.*" I grit my teeth and have to push the word out. I feel her slouch against me, like she's giving up. I won't let her. "These are your friends and they will do everything they can to help you."

"I know. I just don't think they can help me."

"I can, but you won't let me."

"I don't want to owe you anything, Nate. I don't want that to tarnish our relationship."

She slowly slides down my body, takes my hand, and pulls me out towards the bar where everyone is waiting for us.

Laying it on the Line

Jennifer

"Hi, guys," I say, sitting at the table next to Nate. "I need to tell you all something. I need some help, but I don't think you can help me."

"You know we will always try and help any of our girls. You're family to us," Whiskey says.

Spence brings us drinks before he sits down next to Snow. She smiles at him and he takes her hand. I want the type of love they have. I want that all-consuming, can't think of anyone else type of love. Nate could give me that. He *does* give me that.

"Thanks, Whiskey. I really appreciate it. I know I'm still the new girl around here and I don't want to bring trouble to your doorstep."

"Listen, we've been through a lot together. Some of

us more than others, but we look out for each other and it bonds us together even tighter," Sawyer says, smiling at me.

I take a sip of my drink, take a deep breath, and start telling them my story. I tell them about my parents and what their plan is. Everyone is disgusted that my parents would entertain doing that to their only daughter.

"They don't deserve to be parents," Snow says, shaking her head.

"I know, and I don't know what I did to deserve them either." I get choked up and Nate leans over and pulls me in closer.

"Duchess, it'll be fine. We will sort it out. If anyone can sort it out then these guys can." He kisses me on the forehead.

"So, let me get this straight. We've got two months to get them to change their mind about marrying you off?" Sawyer asks.

"Yes."

"What if I marry you that day instead? Would that work?" Nate says.

"What? You want to marry me?"

"We love each other. I know it's early in our relationship, but if it helps you then I'm happy to marry you. I have money so that would keep your parents happy."

I tear up. "Nate, I can't believe you would do that, but when I get married, I want to do it because I love the person and want to spend the rest of my life with them. I would hate to marry you because you feel sorry for me. I want to marry you because you love me and can't live without me."

"I do love you and I don't want to live without you. That's why you're moving in tomorrow."

Someone clears their throat. My head spins and I realise that we aren't alone and everyone is looking at us.

"Sorry," I mumble.

"Don't worry about it. You're both worried and Nate will do anything to keep you safe and happy. We need to work out how we can stop this from happening," Sawyer says.

We throw around a few ideas and then Spence says, "What about getting some publicity. A kind of reverse psychology thing."

"What do you mean?" Nate asks.

"I don't know the ins and outs, but I'm sure Pinkie's parents would be embarrassed if the country knew what they're doing."

"They sure would," I say.

"So, we launch a media campaign highlighting what they want to do and get the country behind you to stop the sham of a wedding," Spence says, and I can feel my hairs standing up on end, giving me goose bumps. He is giving me hope. I look at Nate and he's smiling. He obviously thinks this might work too.

Sawyer claps his hands. "I know just the person who can create that storm, but Nate, you're not going to like it."

Nate's gorgeous face darkens. "Drew," he says, grinding his teeth.

I touch his leg. "If you don't want him to help me then it's fine. I understand."

He takes my face in his hands. "I will do whatever it takes to stop you marrying some arsehole you don't even know. I know that Drew is the right man for the job. But if he so much as touches you or looks at you in any other way than professionally, I will personally kick his arse."

I love when he's territorial. It makes me realise how much he loves me.

"He won't touch her," Sawyer says, reaching for his phone. "I will make sure of it. He just wants her to be happy, and as long as you make her happy then we're all good." He starts to dial a number on his phone.

I lean in to Nate and whisper, "I love you, Nate. I never had feelings for Drew like I do for you." I kiss him gently and feel more emotion than with a powerful kiss.

He smiles when he pulls away then lifts me up and

places me on his lap. He wraps his arms around me. "I can't wait for you to move in tomorrow."

We haven't agreed anything yet, but as always, he goes ahead and pretends we've discussed it and came up with the idea together. I laugh because there is really no point arguing with him. He has my heart–lock, stock, and barrel.

Sawyer stands up and moves away from the table. I can hear him talking to Drew.

"Yeah, buddy. She needs your help... I know you would...When can you get here?... See you then, and Drew? Thank you. I owe you one."

He comes back to the table. "It's settled. Drew is flying out tomorrow morning and we will meet him here tomorrow night after the show. He says he will do whatever it takes to make sure you don't have to get married."

I let out the breath I'm holding. "Thank you so much. I can't believe you're all so willing to help me. I've never met so many kind people."

After chatting for another half an hour or so, Nate stands and says, "Come on, duchess. I need to take you home and show you why you should move in." He smiles and grabs my hand, pulling me up. I crash into his large chest and moan.

"I can't wait to hear more of your moaning later," he whispers in my ear.

I giggle.

"Don't do that or we won't make it home. Remember, we can go use the storeroom if you like, but what I want to do to you is not suitable for the storeroom."

I try not to laugh, but he turns me on so much.

"Right, let's go then, because I can't hold on much longer before I whip your cock out and ride you all the way home."

His face lights up. "See you guys, tomorrow," he says, dragging me out of the club. I can hear everyone laughing behind us as the door closes.

I don't know how we make it home with our clothes still on, but we do. He takes me to his place, and as soon as the door is closed, he pushes me up against the wall. He lifts me up so

I'm straddling his hips and I wrap my legs around his waist. He starts grinding against me.

"Oh my God, Nate. I want you to ride me hard. I need to know how much you love me."

He growls at me. "You don't realise how much I want to be balls deep inside you right now." He pushes his cock against me. I smile, thinking of the pleasure he's going to give me.

He storms up the stairs to the master bedroom and throws me on the bed. He starts to take my clothes off.

When we're both naked, I get ready for hot and furious fucking.

He leans over me and kisses me with so much passion I can feel it all the way to my toes. When he lifts his head, his eyes look different; they're sparkling He gives a mischievous grin and then slowly makes his way down my body, kissing every single inch of me.

"Nate, please fuck me."

He laughs and it sends vibrations straight to my pussy.

"God, Nate, you can be annoying some..." I trail off when his lips wrap around one nipple while his finger and thumb pinch the other one. I arch my back.

"Shush, duchess. You are going to need to save your energy. This is going to take some time and you're going to come at least three times before I do!"

I feel hot all over just thinking about what he's going to do to me to give me three orgasms. He reaches over to his bedside drawer and pulls out some black silk ribbon. My eyes go wide and then he sits up.

"What are you going to do with that, Nate?" I ask nervously.

"I want to tie you to my bed so that you can't wriggle or move. It will make this all so much more fun."

He doesn't wait for me to agree or disagree, he just

takes my wrist and gently wraps the ribbon around it and then brings it up to the headboard post and ties it around it. It's still loose which is good, because I was starting to panic. He takes the other wrist and then does the same.

He sits back on his knees and looks at me. He takes about five minutes just to look at me up and down. His smile gets bigger and bigger.

I start wriggling my arse and trying to thrust my pussy up to him to get some friction. I need to release.

"Duchess, take your time. We have all night. I want to love you. All of you," he says, licking his lips.

He slides back down and then his face is between my legs. I love when he kisses me there.

He slides his hands under my arse and slightly tilts my hips so he has easier access to my pussy. Then he lies there just looking at it. The longer he looks at it, the wetter I get.

It is really an intimate feeling when someone is giving your pussy so much attention and they're not even touching it.

"Nate... please..."

"What, duchess? Tell me what you want."

I try to lift my hips to move my pussy closer to his lips. He smiles and shakes his head. He blows onto my pussy and it makes me gasp.

"I want you to lick me. I want you to eat my pussy."

He chuckles. "My duchess's command is my pleasure!"

However, he doesn't rush to do it like I thought he would. He takes his fucking time about even putting is tongue on me for the first time.

It's so gentle, I'm not sure I even felt it. Then I feel it. He eats me with so much force you'd think he was starving. I buck my back and push my pussy closer to his face, which really isn't possible, but I try.

After what seems like a year, I start screaming his name and bucking up and down. I need my hands to balance myself.

He chuckles then works his way back up my body, paying great attention to my nipples. Kissing me, he forces his tongue in between my lips. He's hungry for me. While he's kissing me, he holds my head between his hands.

His cock is teasing my entrance, and while he's sucking my tongue, he pushes his way in in one thrust.

"Nate," I say into his mouth.

"I know, duchess. I know."

He painstakingly slowly pulls out and then thrusts back in. At the same time, he pulls himself up my body and releases the ties around my wrist. I pull my arms down. They're stiff and sore but the pain is more pleasurable than I thought.

"Seeing you tied up does things to me, duchess, but

I want to feel your hands touch me. I want to feel you run your nails down my back, and I want you to grab my arse and push my cock back inside because you can't wait any longer for me to be deep inside."

I smile at him, throw my hands to his arse, and claw at him. "Move!" I grunt at him.

He chuckles. "Yes, duchess."

He takes his time making love to me and it's the most beautiful and emotional thing I've ever experienced.

We come at the same time and he lies on top of me, panting. "I love you, duchess," he says, kissing the end of my nose.

"I love you too, Nate. I really, really do."

As he rolls off me, he scoops me up and pulls me close so that his front is moulded around my back. I feel the tears start to fall one by one down my face.

I love him so much that I'm desperate not to lose him.

I lie in bed, listening to Pinkie snore gently as I slowly unwrap myself from around her. I can't believe how quickly she has worked her way underneath my skin. I've never slept with the same girl twice. I've never had a girl up to my apartment, and yet here I am living, with the most amazingly beautiful, funniest girl I've ever met.

I am fiercely protective of her and I want her to be happy, but I don't want her to marry this guy her parents are trying to marry her off to.

I walk down the stairs and into the lounge then pour myself a straight whiskey and sit on the balcony. I hate that we have to involve Drew, but he's the best in the business, and if anyone can spin this story, he can.

I like Drew. I've always liked him. But knowing he had his cock inside her tears me up inside. If he even looks at her crooked I won't be able to help myself, and I know I need to rein it in where he's concerned or she'll have my balls.

I smile as I take a sip of my drink. I don't want to lose her from my life. She makes my life so much better.

I finish my drink and wander back up to the bedroom. I stand at the bottom of the bed for a few minutes and just watch her sleeping. The best feeling in the world is slipping under the covers, pulling her back towards me, and hearing her say, "Mmm. Love you, Nate."

"Love you too," I say as I start to drift off to sleep.

The Plan

Pinkie

Two days later, we're finishing the show when I spot Drew at the bar, talking to Spence. I have mixed feelings about seeing him again. Our relationship was intense the times he was here. Now I've had Nate, I don't want anyone else. I smile at Drew and he waves at me.

After we've changed, we head over to the bar and Drew smiles and pulls me in for a hug. "Hey, babe. How are you? I missed you." He kisses me on the cheek.

"Hey, Drew. Thanks for coming over to do this for me. I really need your help."

"You know I would help you any time." I take the

seat next to him and we talk about what he's been doing since I saw him last.

I feel Nate before I see him. He slides in next to me and wraps his arm around my back. "Drew," he says, nodding his head. Pulling me closer, he kisses me on the lips, sucking my bottom lip into his mouth. I know he's claiming me in front of Drew and I let him. It feels right and I lean into him while he talks to Drew.

When the customers have gone, everyone sits around the table and we all have a few drinks. Some of the girls leave until there is only Nate, Drew, Sawyer, Whiskey, Spence, Snow and me.

Spence brings us some drinks and then the conversation turns serious. Sawyer tells Drew what has been going on so that he's up to date with everything.

He looks at me. "Pinkie, I can't believe you're going through this. It's not right. Your parents shouldn't be treating you like this. This is not the Victorian ages."

Nate pulls me closer to him, obviously not happy with Drew looking at me the way he is.

"I can't believe they're doing this to me either. I don't want to marry Jonathan. I want to be with Nate."

"I know," Drew says. "I'm here to make your parents' life a living hell. So this is what I'm going to do."

He spends the next half an hour telling us about the campaign he is going to start. He will tell the media what's going on in the Hamilton Wade household. How my parents are trying to marry me off to keep money in the family. My parents are so well-known that any publicity will not be seen in a favourable light.

"Thank you so much, Drew. I really appreciate it."

"No problem, babe. Anything to help you." He winks at me and Nate growls.

I laugh and turn to face him. "Did you just growl at me?" I whisper, laughing.

"Yes, I did. I don't like him winking at you."

"Oh for God's sake, Nate. You're taking me home tonight and every night. Drew is here to help me."

His face softens. "I'm sorry. I just feel territorial over you. It's a new feeling for me." He reaches out and touches my cheek. I lean into his touch.

"Come on," I say. "Let's get out of here and you can remind me how much you love me."

His face lights up at the thought of fucking me. I love that look.

He stands up and takes my hand, pulling me up. "Drew, it was good to catch up, and thank you so much for helping Pinkie. We really do appreciate it." He offers his hand to Drew to shake.

Drew accepts it and I know they will be fine. Nate puts his hand on the base of my back and guides me out of the club.

"Just wait 'til I get you home, duchess. I am going to fuck you senseless."

I look at him. "Promises, promises."

He laughs at me and winks. "I never renege on a promise."

WHISKEY

We wait until Nate and Pinkie have left before turning our attention to Drew.

"So, what do you think her chances are of not marrying this Jonathan guy? Do you think they can really cut her off and sue her for the money she has spent these last few months? Are they willing to lose her because of it?" Sawyer asks.

Drew shakes his head. "It's going to be tough. Whatever we put out there, the press are going to find out she works here. Are you guys happy to have your club brought into this? You've built up a really good reputation."

I look at Sawyer. He nods at me. He gave me the reins a few years ago and he's leaving the decision up to me.

"When I was down and out, destitute and at my lowest point in my life, I found Whiskey Sour. It's been like a beacon for other girls who are suffering or have been through traumatic experiences. We don't advertise that fact, but each of the Whiskey Sour girls has been through something harrowing in their lives. Pinkie is just another girl we will look after, and if Whiskey Sour gets dragged into the press, then that it is what it takes." I feel passionately about my club, but the girls are more important to me.

"I thought you would say that," Drew says, smiling at me. "Now, get me another drink and I will start on the plan tomorrow. Tonight, we party!"

We laugh. Drew is a party animal, but he's the most loyal man you could meet. He is very passionate about Whiskey Sour and has been on board from the beginning. I know how much he thinks of Pinkie and he will do whatever it takes to help her.

We sit drinking with Drew for another couple of hours until we're the only ones left.

"Right, that's me done," Drew says, looking at his watch. "I'm still working on US time. Sorry, guys."

"It's okay. Whiskey and I always stay until everyone leaves. We like to be here when it's silent. It's not very often during the night we get a chance to just look around and be proud of what we've achieved," Sawyer says, touching my leg. He grips my thigh and squeezes.

Drew looks at us then laughs. "That's my cue to

leave. I'm not staying to watch you two fuck each other with your eyes or any other parts of your bodies."

We both laugh at him and we follow him when he stands and walks out to the entrance area. "Shall we call you a taxi, Drew?" I ask.

"No, thanks. I'm going to walk some of the way and hail one. It's a lovely morning and I have a lot to think about."

I hug him, and he hugs me back tightly. "Thank you so much, Drew. You know how much we appreciate your help."

"You're very welcome. You know how much I like Pinkie and how much I love you guys."

We watch him walk away then we close the door and walk back inside, locking up behind us.

"Princess, I love you," Sawyer says, guiding me back into the club.

"I love you too."

"You know how you'd do anything to make me happy?" he says, smirking and waggling his eyebrows.

"Yes," I say tentatively.

"Will you dance for me?"

"I dance for you most nights, Sawyer. In the bedroom."

"I know you do, princess, but I want you to dance on the stage. I'm sure I can find some music in Nate's booth."

"Come on then," I say as he takes my hand and pulls me into Nate's booth.

He turns on the light and I start giggling.

"What are you laughing at?" he asks, staring at me.

"I'm just wondering how many times Nate and Pinkie have had sex in here. We could do it in here. I'd love to wind him up with pictures," I say, laughing uncontrollably.

"Princess, you are evil. But I have bigger and better plans for you tonight." He presses a button and some music plays. "Get on that stage and be ready to take your clothes off for me, princess."

I love when he bosses me around. It really turns me on. I kiss him quickly on the lips and then skip out of the booth and head towards the stage.

I stand in the darkness and wait to see what he plays. I can feel the hairs standing up on my arms. The anticipation is exhilarating. I stopped dancing about two years ago. Now and again I get back on the stage, but mostly I just dance for Sawyer. He is my everything.

I hear the deep, dulcet tones of Etta James singing *Tough Lover*. As she starts to sing, he turns the lights up to highlight me on the stage. I move to the beat of the music, swaying, jutting one hip out then the other one. I move very slowly around the stage, removing my clothes until the last *Tough Lover* when I stand naked with my arm up in the air. He turns out the spotlight and it's silent.

My heart is beating so fast, with the adrenaline shooting through me from dancing again in addition to the thought that Sawyer is watching me, and I know he's on his way over to me.

By the time he hits the stage, he too is naked. "I'll be your tough lover any day, princess." He growls as he makes his way towards me. As soon as his hand touches me, I feel safe and jump up to capture him between my legs. I wrap them around his waist and he moves me to the back wall on the stage. He pushes me against the wall and, perfectly timed by him, a spotlight shines on us. Everything else is in complete darkness except us and what we're doing.

I love Whiskey Sour and everything it represents. Am I worried that this mess with Pinkie is going to go against us? No, not at all. We aren't in the dark ages anymore, we will be behind her every step of the way. She's one of ours now. She's family and we do everything we can for our Whiskey Sour family.

Media Frenzy

Everywhere I look, my name is in the paper. There are pictures of me as Jennifer, in my twinset and pearls, and there are pictures of me as Pinkie in my sexy outfits and pink hair. I know which pictures I prefer.

My family have been trashed and humiliated for the last month. I haven't heard from them, but I know Drew has. He came to the apartment a week ago and sat down with Nate and me and explained how things were going.

"Look, you both need to know what I've organised. It's going to go viral. You're both going to be in demand for interviews and Whiskey Sour is going to be busy. You're lucky they have such a strict membership policy. I've spoken to Whiskey and she has agreed that they're not taking any new members for the foreseeable future until they know this media circus has calmed

down. They need to make sure the members are real members and not just interested in writing about your story."

"Oh my God," I say, gasping. "I never thought about how it would affect Whiskey Sour. Whiskey must hate me right now."

"Don't worry. Whiskey is doing well out of this, but her main interest is you and making sure that you are okay and don't have to go through with the marriage."

"So, how's the campaign looking for Pinkie? Are her parents backing down at all?"

Drew shakes his head. "Unfortunately not. They came out at the very start of this campaign and gave their view that this is a family tradition and they have a familial obligation to see it through with their child. They aren't budging and it doesn't seem to make any difference that the rest of the UK and the press are in your corner," he says, looking at me.

"This isn't what we want to hear." Nate takes my hand in his. He squeezes it, reminding me that he's here for me and he isn't going anywhere.

"I know, Nate, and you know how much I'm working to get the right result. The last thing I want is for her to marry someone she doesn't love. She is such a passionate woman and she needs to be with someone who can nurture that, like you."

My parents haven't made any more statements and

have refused to be interviewed. I've dragged their name though the mud and yet they still stand by their beliefs.

We haven't heard anything from them and my 'wedding day' is getting closer. Every day, I open my post box with trepidation, not knowing what it's going to hold.

I've become snappy, angry, and so anxious that I know I'm not a nice person to live with. I'm just hoping and praying that Drew's campaign works and I can go about living my life.

"Morning, duchess," Nate says, nuzzling into my neck.

He kisses below my ear and then trails his tongue up to my earlobe.

"Mmm, morning," I groan as I turn my head to catch his lips with mine.

"Did you sleep?" he asks when he breaks free of my grasp.

"I got a few hours." I've not been sleeping too well because my mind is always turning. When I close my eyes, all I can see is me walking down the aisle in a beautiful dress, and when the groom turns, it's Jonathan. It makes me wake up in a cold sweat. I don't want to spend my life with someone who doesn't love me. I want the passion, excitement, unconditional love that Nate gives me. The thoughts of not seeing him weigh heavily on my mind.

"Duchess, don't be so sad. Look, I have a meeting today with my solicitor about some financial issues, but I might have a surprise for you when I get back. Just remember, I love you so much. I'll do everything to make this better."

"What are you up to?" I ask, kissing the end of his nose.

"Patience, duchess. Have some patience."

He rolls me over so he's on top of me. "I love you. Let me love you. Please?"

I let him make love to me. It's hot and passionate, but slow and emotional. Both of us pouring our emotions into our lovemaking. It feels like the last time we're going to do it. I have tears running down my face when I come.

"Duchess, I won't let you marry him. We can elope at any time."

"I know, but then I'll be getting sued and all the negativity surrounding us will eat us both up and you'll hate me and I can't let that happen." I hold onto his body tightly. I don't want to let go.

"I won't hate you, duchess. I could never hate you."

My phone ring, and when I look at the screen, I see it's my mother. I show Nate and he tries to take the phone from me. I shake my head. I need to answer it. I need to know what they have to say for themselves.

"Hi, Mother," I say with no emotion.

"Jennifer. You need to come home now. This has gone on long enough. Your wedding is in one week and there are lots of things to sort out."

"Oh my God. I can't believe you're still going ahead with this. I know you hate me, but this is preposterous."

"We don't hate you, Jennifer. We love you and want you to have the best in your life."

"What if I have the best now? It's not good enough for you. All you and Father want is more money. Money doesn't make anyone happy, Mother!"

She laughs, a frigid, evil laugh. "Jennifer, are you serious? You think what you have with that... that... man is the best in life? He's a disc jockey, for God's sake. He is a womaniser and he will soon tire of you and move on. What are you going to do then? You'll have no money, no friends, and no life. Are you telling me you would give up everything for that kind of life?"

He *was* a player, but he's not now. I see him looking at me. He's trying to listen to the call.

She carries on talking, wearing me down. She thinks she has won and that I'm starting to believe her. I don't, but I do have doubts in my mind.

"Jennifer, we have a meeting today and then I expect you home tomorrow. We have a lot to plan and only a few days to do it." She hangs up the phone. No discussion, just my instruction to go home.

I sigh.

"What did she say, Pinkie?" Nate says as he tips my chin up to look at him. The tears in my eyes start to overflow. He shakes his head. "No. No way! You can't go through with this. What about me? What about how I feel about you? You've changed my life, Pinkie. I can't be without you. I love you. I can give you the passion and love that you talk about. We have that already."

"I know, Nate. I know."

I climb out of bed and walk into the bathroom to have a shower. I don't talk or look in his direction. I need time to think.

After I've showered, dressed, and composed myself, I walk into the kitchen to find a continental breakfast laid out for me. Nate is smiling and pulls out the chair for me to sit. He leans down and plants a light kiss on my lips.

"Today for breakfast, madame," he says in a French accent, "we have croissants, pain au chocolat, and Bucks Fizz."

I laugh. "Bucks Fizz. You're pushing the boat out a bit, aren't you?"

"Anything for you, duchess."

Breakfast is gorgeous and we laugh and joke, forgetting about the emotional phone call I just had.

"I think I might go and see Scottie today, have a

chat with him. Is that okay? I know you said you have a meeting today and then we're both working tonight."

He eyes me suspiciously but nods his head. "Of course, duchess."

"What time does your meeting finish?"

"About five, depending on the outcome." He pulls me into a hug and wraps his arms around me. He rests his chin on my head. "You know I love you and will do anything for you, right?"

"I do."

I gasp. Those are the words I will be saying to someone else in less than a week. I just about hold back the tears long enough to look up at him and meet his lips with a passionate kiss.

He groans. "I need to stop doing this or neither of us will get out this afternoon."

I laugh and we go about tidying the kitchen and getting ready. We both leave at the same time and I call Scottie to let him know I'm on my way.

"Hey, Scottie. I missed you so much. I'm on my way over. I really need someone to talk to."

"Hey, Pinkie! Mi casa es tu casa!"

"Cool. I'll be there in about half an hour."

I hang up, and Nate and I walk to Piccadilly Circus to catch trains in different directions. We hug before we go but things are strained between us. I need to make a decision quickly. I'm hoping Scottie will be able to shed some light and help me.

NATE

When I leave Pinkie at Piccadilly Circus, she looks so lost and confused. I worry that this is all becoming too much for her, but I don't give up without a fight. From the emotions this morning, I know I'm about to have the biggest fight of my life. I need to keep her. I can't let her marry anyone else.

I lied a little when I said that I was going to see my solicitor. I'm actually going to see her parents, with my solicitor. I don't like doing this behind her back, but I know she wouldn't want me to see them and have to listen to the crap that they're spouting. I heard her mum on the phone this morning, trying to get her to change her mind. Trying to turn her against me. I won't stand for it.

I meet Paul, my solicitor, at the Tube station then we walk to their house. I'm excited to see where Pinkie was brought up, but scared in case she goes ape shit when she hears what I'm about to do.

"Fuck. Look at the size of this house. You weren't

joking when you said they were loaded," I say to Paul as we stand at the gate, waiting to be let in.

"I know. This family is huge, Nathanial."

"It's Nate. Please don't call me that. You know how much I hate it."

He laughs. We walk towards the front door, taking in the landscape around us. This is a very well kept house and I start to get a feel of her family and how different to them she is. Any person living here would be stuffy and boring; nothing like my duchess.

After ringing the bell, the front door opens and a tall man in his late sixties opens the door. "Gentlemen, come in."

We walk past him and stand in the hallway.

"If you'll follow me, the office is down here off the vestibule."

What the fuck is a vestibule? We follow him anyway.

When we're shown into the office, I see a lady who looks a little bit like Pinkie, except she's very cold-looking. The man who brought us to this room stands beside her and puts his arm around her waist.

"I'm Leonard and this is Emily." They both hold out their hands to be shaken.

I take his hand and shake it firmly. I don't like limp handshakes; it means someone is weak-willed. I shake

Pinkie's mother's hand and hers is even stronger. It tells me who is the real leader in this family.

They show us to some seats and then they both sit behind the desk. Her father is first to speak. "So, Nathanial, to what do we owe this pleasure? Whatever could you want to talk to us about?"

I smirk. "I might as well get to the point. I love your daughter and I want to marry her. I'm here today to offer you my money in exchange for your daughter."

Her mum gasps and her husband looks at her. "Well, this is unexpected." He turns back to look at me and all I see is disgust written on his face. He looks at me like I'm a bad smell or something.

"I'm kind of old-fashioned and wanted to ask you, her loving parents, for her hand in marriage before I ask her. That's tradition, right?"

Her mother laughs. "Yes, it's tradition, but not in this house. We marry for money. The idea of our family name continuing in one form or another is the aim of marriage. All this marrying for love is codswallop."

"Well, you might not have married for love, but that's what your daughter wants to do. So what if she breaks tradition? They are there to be broken."

"Well, we might consider it," her father says, taking his wife's hand in his. "For the right price. But we very much doubt you can afford the sum we have in mind."

"Try me. You might be surprised," I say, as the tension in my body gets even tighter.

"When Jonathan marries *Jennifer*, he will be bringing a few million into our family business. Not just that, he has property both here and abroad, a yacht, and a lot more than you could ever have."

I squirm. That is a lot.

"So, theoretically, if I could give you, say, three million to stop this farce from happening, you wouldn't lose out."

"Financially, no, we wouldn't lose out. But reputation-wise, yes, we would. You see, Jonathan's family has a lot of clout in the business world and that is the main reason we're letting him marry our daughter."

"What about her happiness? Does that not mean anything to you? She's your daughter, for Christ's sake!" Paul reaches over and places his hand on my arm to calm me down.

I lean over to him. "Paul, what do you think I should do? I have the money to give them. I would do anything for her. Do you think they still won't let me marry her?" I whisper so they can't hear me.

"It's up to you. That's an awful lot of money and I know you have it, but your trust fund will be seriously depleted."

"I don't care. I want to marry her. I want to love her like she needs to be loved and I don't want to lose her."

Paul sits up and faces her parents. "Nate agrees that if she doesn't marry Jonathan, you cancel the wedding then he will pay all the money that you are going to sue her for. After that, she won't have anything to do with her family and she won't find out that he paid it off. You will be able to tell her that you changed your minds. At least it will restore some of her faith in humanity."

Emily laughs. I don't know what she thinks is funny, because right now, all I want to do is punch them both.

"You haven't included a second option. That Jennifer *will* marry Jonathan, they *will* live happily ever after and *you* won't be in the picture. Since all the media hype you have decided to bring to our doorstep, this marriage has to go ahead so everyone knows we mean business. There will be a clause in their agreement that they can't divorce for at least ten years. That should give them long enough to develop feelings for each other. They might even love each other by then. I'm sure they will be having children straight away, as that is in the agreement too."

She's mocking me and I stand and stride to their desk. I thump my hands down on it and lean over the desk towards Emily. "You think you run this show, don't you? Well, what you need to realise is that Pinkie runs this show. Without her, there will be no wedding. Without her, you won't get that money. Without her, you don't progress in this world. Maybe you should have thought about that before you started to push her away."

Paul puts a hand on my shoulder. "Sit down, Nate. Getting angry isn't going to help."

I take a seat and stare at these two disgusting people.

"However large your offer, we will have to refuse it. You don't fit the criteria for our daughter."

"Criteria? You have a fucking criteria for your daughter? You make me sick, the pair of you!"

Paul says, "Nate!"

I turn to look at him. "What? I don't give a fuck anymore. They are willing to sell their daughter to the highest bidder and they don't even take her feelings into it." I turn to look at them again. "You are seriously fucked up and I hope it all blows up in your face."

I stand and grab Paul's arm to pull him up. "We're out of here," I say to no one in particular, and walk out of the office, out the front door, and down the drive.

I am so mad, I could seriously hit something right now. We walk until we reach the first pub, and after downing two whiskeys, I can finally speak. "I can't fucking believe it. I really thought it would work and they would buy it. I thought they would take my money and let me keep her."

"I know. I thought so too. It's more about reputation for them now. Drew has almost annihilated their family and they don't intend to back down now. They feel that by backing down, they have lost. They could have easily taken your money and this could be over, but they're too stubborn to do that."

"What am I going to do now, Paul? This was my last hope."

"I don't know, Nate. I really don't."

We have another drink and then my phone rings. When I look at the screen, I see it's Scottie.

"Yo, dude. What's up?"

"Nate, you need to get down here. Your woman is pissed as a fart and she is talking rubbish. She won't listen to me, but you need to get your arse over her immediately!"

"On my way. Keep her there and tell her I love her."

I look at Paul. "I have to go, mate. Pinkie needs me."

"You go to your woman, and when you know what you want to do, just let me know. I'm behind you one hundred percent."

"Thanks, Paul. I appreciate it." I shake his hand and then give him a one-handed man hug.

I hail a cab outside the pub and make my way over to Scottie's house.

When I get there, Pinkie has left. He invites me in. "Nate, she's gone. She's gone to see Whiskey. You need to leave her to speak to her alone. Let's have a drink and a chat. I know you're planning something and I know just what we need to do."

"Tell me more."

FINAL SHOW

PINKIE

I'm sitting in Whiskey Sour with Whiskey on one side and Sawyer on the other. Drew is on his way over and I'm avoiding Nate. I hate that I'm pushing him away, but I know what I have to do.

"So you're going to go through with the wedding? Am I hearing this right?" Whiskey asks incredulously.

"It's the only thing I can do. I can't afford to pay them back their money. I don't want to get sued because then my life will be hell and Nate will start to hate me for bringing all this shit into his life. I might as well be miserable. At least then he will have a chance to be happy again." I sob. The thought of Nate with another woman kills me.

"I've not said anything to either of you about this, but I know that the money isn't an issue. Between all of us, we can help you with that," Sawyer says.

"I couldn't do that to any of you. Thank you, but I don't want to build friendships and lives on loans."

Whiskey pushes a drink in front of me. "Drink this. Don't make any rash decisions Pinkie."

"Look, between David, Stig, Spencer and me, we can always find some dirt on your family, something that would blow up in the media and discredit them. It's a big thing to do, but you're halfway there already. You just have to say the word and we'll make all this disappear." Sawyer leans across the table and puts his hand on top of mine. He looks after us girls. He's like a father figure to us all. I can feel tears forming again.

"Thank... thank you so much, Sawyer. You don't know how much that means to me. Maybe one day I'll be back knocking on your door, asking you to do that for me, but I think, this week, I need to fight my own battles."

"The offer stands whenever you want us to do it."

"Does this mean you're leaving us?" Whiskey asks with uncertainty.

"I haven't said anything to Nate yet, but I need to go home tomorrow. This wedding is happening on Saturday whether I want it to or not, so I need to start preparing myself for my new life. Tonight will be the end of Pinkie and the beginning of Jennifer again. Although, I don't think I will ever be the same Jennifer I was a year ago."

"You know Nate isn't going to find this easy. He loves you and he would do anything to make you happy," Whiskey says.

"I know. He said we could elope and just shut ourselves away from the world, but that wouldn't be the kind of life he would want full time. He needs music, he needs women, and he needs Whiskey Sour."

"He needs you, Pinkie," Sawyer says, looking over my head.

I turn to see what he's looking at but I already know. I felt him walk into the room.

"I need you, duchess. But if this is what you think you need to do then I love you enough to let you go." He stands behind me and puts his hand on my shoulder.

I can't breathe right now. He's going to let me go. He knows I'm going to do this and he's not going to stand in my way. I stand and walk into his open arms, sobbing.

This is what heartbreak feels like. My heart has just shattered into tiny pieces and no one is going to be able to ever glue it back together again.

"Give me tonight to love you, duchess. Please? Tomorrow is another day and you can go and do whatever you need to do. I understand and can't stop you. But I want tonight so you won't forget me for a long time."

"Thank you, Nate. Tonight is about us. Tonight is about our family," I say, looking at Whiskey and Sawyer.

After I have composed myself, the four of us sit and drink until the girls start arriving for the show. Beau follows them in and stands next to me with his arms crossed. "Drinking before work! Pinkie, you need to take your job seriously or you won't be able to dance here anymore."

I burst out laughing and he just looks at me.

"What did I say that was so funny?" he says, moving his hands to his hips.

"Tonight is my last night. I'm leaving. I have to go and marry some ignorant, stuck up fucker and live unhappily ever after." I try to be sarcastic to hide my emotions, but I don't think I'm doing a good job.

"Oh no, babe. I'm sorry. You know I was only joking. You can't leave. We all need you here. You're family!" He leans down to hug me and he sniffles into my shoulder.

The girls all heard too and they're crying and hugging me too.

Eventually, Beau steps away and looks over to Nate. "Hey, big boy. If you don't know what to do with your cock when she's gone, then I'll always help you out." He winks at him. I can't help myself; I laugh.

Nate says, "Fuck you, Beau."

"That's exactly what I was thinking." He laughs.

It sets us all off. Spence and Snow come in and they see what's going on. Spence gets us all our signature drinks and we have a toast to family.

All the girls leave to get ready for the show and Nate pulls me to one side. "I love you and I know you need to do this. I'm not happy about it but I do love you enough. Tonight though, I am going to find you when you least expect it and I'm going to fuck you whenever, wherever I want. Deal?"

I'm not sure if he's asking me or telling me. "Deal!" I smile as he reaches out to shake my hand. "Bring it on!"

"Oh, I intend to! Now, go get changed. You don't want to let the girls down." He slaps my arse as I walk away.

When I open the door to the dressing room, the girls are all waiting for me. "Oh, Pinkie. You aren't really leaving, are you?" Baby says.

"Yeah. Tell us it's not true," Dee Dee adds.

"Sorry, girls. It's true. I have to go back home and marry some douchebag. You've all seen the papers so you know what's been going on. I'm going to miss you all so much. You're like my sisters."

They pull me into a group hug. "We will miss you too, Pinkie," Sissy says.

Beau claps his hands. "Come on, ladies. That's enough of that sobbing. Let's get this show on the road."

We all separate and move to our dressing tables. We each have one of those large mirrors with lights all around them and a table top at the bottom. I love it, and when I sit at my stool, I look into the mirror and smile. I love this life. I apply my make-up and get ready for my last show.

NATE

The girls put on a fantastic show. I was a little bit naughty during freeplay because I chose *Listen To Your Heart* by Roxette. I wanted the words to say something to Pinkie. The way I did when I first met her.

Her dance was absolutely breath-taking and I could see she had tears in her eyes. She knew what I was doing.

I can't believe I just told her I'm letting her go.

That was the hardest thing I have ever had to do. I need her to believe that I'll let her go. It's the only thing I can do for my plan to work.

When I met Scottie the other day, we made some plans, and even though it breaks my heart for her to leave, I need to do it.

After the show, I wait for the girls to start coming out of the dressing room, and when I know that only Pinkie is left, I wait outside the door. I've turned the lights off, and when she opens the door, I pin her to the wall. "Did you enjoy the show, duchess?"

Her breathing quickens. "I did."

"I hear you're getting married to an arsehole. Is he going to be man enough for you?"

"No," she says, sounding sad.

"Are you going to remember this feeling?" I ask as I pin her to the wall using my crotch. My cock is rigid and straining for release.

"I'll never forget how your cock feels inside me." She sighs.

I reach down and run my hand under the waistband of her knickers until I reach her sweet spot. "You're so wet. Always so wet for me." I slide my finger in between her lips and hear her groan.

She reaches back and squeezes my cock through my jeans. "Do you still think it's a cocktail sausage?" I laugh, remembering what she said to me the first time I accosted her in the corridor.

"This is more than a foot long!" She giggles.

I shuffle her into the disabled toilet, the room where I first made her come. As soon as I've locked the door, she turns to face me, I pull her skirt up, and she wraps her legs around my waist. I free my cock, pull her knickers to one side, and in one swift movement, I'm inside her.

"Nate." I spin us around and she's leaning against the wall.

"Hold tight, duchess. I need to fuck you hard and fast. Any complaints?"

She shakes her head. "No. Fuck me hard."

I go deeper and harder than I have ever gone before.

"Nate, I'm going to come."

"Duchess, come on my cock."

She starts to quiver around my cock and it sends vibrations all the way through me. It sends us both over the edge.

God, I love her. She makes me feel whole. I don't know what I'm going to do when she's gone. I'm going to miss her so much.

When we stop panting, I lean my forehead against hers. She looks into my eyes and I see the tears.

"Don't cry, duchess. Not until you leave me tomorrow."

"I'll try. I promise."

We get dressed and go out to meet the others. The club is closing and I know they want to party. Tonight is for family. Tonight is for Pinkie.

Fourteen

PRELUDE

PINKIE

I wake up with a banging headache and I roll over in the bed, expecting to see Nate. The bed is empty except for a single red rose. I sit up quickly and feel like I'm going to puke.

"Nate?" I shout. "Nate, are you here?"

Nothing. I don't hear anything. I get out of bed and carry the rose with me. There was a note lying under it and I carefully open the envelope to take the card out.

"I choose you.
And I'll choose you
over and over.
Without pause,
Without a doubt,

I'll keep
choosing you!"

I run down the stairs, shouting out his name. But there's no one here. Nate has gone. He's left me. He knew how hard it was going to be for me to leave him today, so he's taken that pain away from me because he loves me.

I make coffee and sit reading his card. What does he mean, he chooses me? I know he does, but I only chose Jonathan because I have to.

I don't have anything to take home with me because Pinkie is no more. From today, I will be Jennifer Hamilton Wade again. Boring, beige, and subservient. The complete opposite of Pinkie.

Leaving the apartment, I glance back and feel the tears coming. I can't let them flow. This was my decision and I have to stick by it. There are only five days until my wedding, and I'm going to be so busy, I won't have time to think about Nate and my Whiskey Sour family.

I hope.

When I walk back into my house, my parents are waiting for me.

"Glad you made the right decision, Jennifer. Those people weren't right for you. Look at all the trouble you've caused to the family," my father says, shaking his head.

I just look at the floor and don't answer back, then I walk up the stairs to my bedroom and throw myself on my bed.

Mother walks in about thirty minutes later. "Jennifer, we need to talk. Your wedding is in five days and we have to get your dress. I have done almost everything else. You just need to come with me today to try on some dresses."

"Whatever. I don't care."

"I know you don't, but you will look like you care. Thanks to your friends, we have the media following us. They want to do a TV programme about you following this."

"I'll do whatever I have to do. Just don't expect me to like it. I'll be showered and changed in an hour. We can go then."

"Perfect. Your appropriate clothes are in your wardrobe." She walks out and closes the door behind her.

I shrug and then go about showering away all traces of Pinkie, her friends, and the best six months of her life.

"Do we have to go into another bridal shop, Mother? I'm bored. There is nothing I like."

"You are being too fussy. I thought you said you would wear whatever."

"I did, but I can't walk down the aisle in some of those dresses, even if the whole thing is a farce."

"Look, I know everything seems bleak right now. I didn't like your father when I married him, but I love him now. He was so loving back in those days and I grew to look forward to seeing him. I wanted to make everything amazing for him. You'll feel like that in a few months' time. I promise."

I mutter under my breath, "I'll never feel like that again."

We walk into Brides With Flair. I hope I find something semi decent in this one because I really don't want to go to another shop.

Looking around, I see that everything is all the same. White, long, tight, ball gown. Nothing stands out, and if I'm only doing this once then I want to be wearing something that shows off me.

My hands touch a pale pink dress and my heart starts to race. I've entered a small section at the back of the shop. It looks like this is where they keep their coloured wedding dresses. I now know that I need a pink wedding dress. How I'm going to get my mother to agree, I don't know, but hell, I am going to try.

The sales assistant sees me looking and comes over. "Do you like the coloured one?"

I nod. "I sure do. Especially pink ones. Can I try some of these on, please?"

"Of course you can. Point out four that you like and we can try them on."

I look up and down the rail and see four that I really like and she takes them to the changing room.

I try the first one on. It's a dusty pink, tight, similar to a bandage dress, except softer. At the knee, it kicks into a mermaid dress. There is a black velvet belt with diamantes on it.

Mother comes over. "You are not wearing a dress that isn't white! Absolutely not."

"Madam," the sales assistant says, "your daughter is getting married and she should be allowed to wear what she wants."

Mother huffs.

"Mother, I am marrying Jonathan, which is what you and Father want me to do. Surely I can pick a dress that I will like and feel happy in. It might be the only happy thing about the whole day."

She looks like she's going to argue, but then she relents. "Your father will kill me."

"Maybe you need to remind him of those days

when he was being romantic and good to you then." I turn and walk back into the changing room to try on the next dress.

On the hanger is a dress that is going to make my mother flip out, but I love it. I step into it as it has a full skirt. It's baby pink at the top, and then on the bustier, it turns into a bright, hot pink. It's tight to the waist and then puffs out to a full skirt with tulle underneath it. The pink is gorgeous and there are small flowers with diamantes in them on the bodice and then in the overlay on the skirt. I look in the mirror and I want to cry. This dress is gorgeous, and it is the wedding dress I should be marrying Nate in, not that fuckwit Jonathan.

I step out of the changing room and Mother stares at me. I know she wants to say something scathing, but I can see tears in her eyes. I think she likes it.

"Mother, this is the one. This is the one I want."

"Your father really is not going to like this, but you're right. You are doing everything else for us, therefore we should let you have the dress of your choice. I will talk to him and straighten it out with him."

"Thanks, Mother." I lean in to hug her, which is a bit awkward because of the dress.

I change back into my dowdy clothes while Mother pays for the dress. Before I walk back out to the shop, the shop assistant comes to find me.

"Listen, I've been watching all the media recently and I'm shocked that you're going through with the wedding."

"I don't really have much choice. They will sue me and bring an awful lot of trouble to my friends and my work place. I can't do that to my friends."

"So, you're willing to sacrifice all your happiness and friendships to keep your parents happy?"

"Yes, but it's more than that. I don't want my friends to suffer because they're friends with me. I can't watch them go through that because of me."

"Well, from what I've seen, I don't think your friends will disown you. You mean too much to them," she says indignantly as she walks out of the dressing room and back to the front of the shop.

I'm shocked she spoke to me like that, and it makes me feel like shit. Am I really doing the right thing? Should I sacrifice my happiness for my parents?

I can't afford to be bankrupt at my age.

"Hurry up, Jennifer. We have to go to the florist now."

We leave the shop and Mother tells me she has arranged for the dress to be dropped to the house after the necessary alterations.

"Now, Jennifer, you need to have a little bit more taste with the flowers. I've given you your own choice of dress, so I'm going to pick the flowers. Something needs to be classy at this wedding!" She storms into the flower shop.

Watching her, I throw my head up to heaven and count to ten before I follow her in.

We get back home about two hours later. She wanted to get lingerie, some presents for some of the guests, and then she took me to some organic vegetarian restaurant for dinner and it was horrible. Firstly, I had to eat all that crap that they served, and secondly, I had to try and make small talk with my Mother–not good.

While I'm lying on my bed, thinking about the wedding, my phone pings with a message.

It's Nate.

Hey duchess. I wasn't going to message you. I wanted you to get on with your life, but I miss you. Xx

I miss you. You weren't there when I woke up xx

I couldn't do the whole goodbye thing. Sorry xx

Me neither xx

**It's going to be strange at work without you.
Can't you sneak out and use your
membership to come visit? X**

**You know I can't. I wouldn't be able to leave
you a second time xx**

Duchess you're killing me xx

I don't reply; it only makes me feel worse.

I don't leave my room all evening because I don't want to spend time with my parents. Scottie, Ruby, and Drew message me, asking me to come back and not to get married. They all tell me the same thing–that I'm making a mistake. I just can't see how I can avoid the wedding.

There is a loud noise thumping on my door, waking me with a start. "What?"

The door opens and my father walks in. He sits on the end of my bed. "Jennifer, where are your manners? We brought you up better than that."

I sigh. "Hello. Father."

"You need to buck your ideas up, young lady. We have spent a lot of money to put this wedding together and all I see in front of me is a sultry, moody teenager. If I thought those days were bad, they are nothing compared to the last six months. You have disgraced your mother and me. You will walk down that aisle and you will smile. Do you hear me?"

"Yes, Father." I bow my head and look at the bed. I hate this person he makes me. I hate myself. I feel weak, and all the fun I had over the last six months slowly ebbs away, leaving me empty and frustrated.

He smiles and then stands and walks away, closing the door behind him. I roll over in bed and cry. I sob so hard it feels like I'm cleansing my soul.

After I get dressed and go downstairs, I hear voices in the office. I walk over quietly so I can find out who's in there.

Standing outside the door, I hear my mother, father, and a third voice. Male. Young. Fuck, it's Jonathan. I listen more intently.

"Sir, are you sure this is going ahead? I've got a lot riding on this marriage."

"Of course it's going ahead," Father says. "Why would you think any different?"

"Have you looked at the newspapers recently? There are polls out there saying she isn't going to be there. Then there are odds that the marriage won't last. Everyone is against this except you and my parents."

I can just picture Jonathan running his fingers under his shirt collar and maybe even loosening his tie.

"This wedding *is* going ahead," my father says. "There will be no talk of it not happening and there is absolutely no way this marriage will not work. Do you hear me, Jonathan?"

"Yes. Yes, sir."

Oh my God, Jonathan is spineless. He can't even argue with my father. How the hell am I going to stay married to this fuckwit?

I knock on the door and don't wait to be invited in. Everyone turns to look at me.

"Jonathan," I say, nodding at him. "What's going on, Father?"

"Nothing you need to be concerned about. We were just discussing work."

Yeah, right. I can't be bothered to argue.

"Jennifer, I came to see if you want to go for lunch with me today. I'd like to get to know you a bit better," Jonathan says.

"Yes, she would love to." My mother answers for me.

"I can speak for myself. I'll go to lunch with you, Jonathan, but don't expect me to enjoy it." I turn to walk away.

"Be ready in fifteen minutes," he says.

I walk out of the office without saying another word.

I arse around in my room for fifteen minutes then take another ten minutes to walk down the stairs.

He's waiting for me when I reach the bottom and

he guides me out of the house with his hand on the bottom of my back. I try to wriggle out of his reach, but he has quite a firm grip on me.

Lunch is awkward as he tries to make small talk. It doesn't help that I'm only giving yes and no answers. When we get to dessert, I lay my spoon down and say, "Why are you doing this? What do you get out of marrying me?"

He blushes. "Well, I get to marry a beautiful woman, of course."

"That is not why you're doing this and we both know it."

"Your family name has been around for generations. For my family and your family to be bonded in business and personal lives is the icing on the cake."

"So this is a business transaction for you?"

"Yes, Jennifer. It is. A business decision." He has the audacity to look smug.

"What about my feelings? Have you thought about my feelings and how this affects me?"

He sits back in his chair and he reminds me of my father. I feel sick.

"Of course I've thought of your feelings. I've thought of nothing else but feeling you." He leans forward. "Pinkie."

I gasp.

"I can't wait for our wedding night when you dance for me on our own."

I push my chair back and stand up. "You have got to be joking. We may be getting married, but it is on paper only. I do not intend to sleep in the same room as you, let alone the same bed, so you had better get that into your thick head."

I start to walk away, but he's quicker than me and grabs hold of my arm then pulls me out into the corridor leading to the toilets.

"Now, listen to me, Jennifer. I will be marrying you and it won't be just in name. You will be sleeping in my bed from Saturday night, and as your husband, I have certain rights that you *will* be fulfilling." I swear he licks his lips.

I pull out of his grasp and run to the toilet. I just make it to the toilet before I vomit everywhere. I have snot and tears running down my face. I really thought this business decision marriage would just be a front and he wouldn't want that side of our marriage. I assumed he would sleep with other women instead of me.

After finishing vomiting, I clean myself up and then I text Scottie.

Scottie, I need you. Can I come over? I need to talk to someone so much xx

I don't wait long for a reply.

Of course babe. I am here for you always.

Thanks see you in a short while. Love you xx

Scottie opens the door when I knock wildly. "Pinkie, come here. I've missed you."

He pulls me into a hug and squeezes me tight. I start sobbing. I thought I had it under control, but obviously not.

He moves to let me in and then closes the door behind me. "Let's go inside and you can tell me all about it."

Pink Wedding

There's a harsh knock on my door. I slowly open my eyes and shout, "I'm awake!"

When the door opens, my parents walk in carrying a tray with breakfast on it.

What the hell is going on? My parents never bring me breakfast in bed.

They make their way over to the bed and sit down on the end.

"Morning, Jennifer. We wanted to make sure you eat today because there won't be much time later on. I'm so excited you're getting married in a few hours. It's going to be a fabulous day. The sun is shining and you are going to be so beautiful," Mother says as she hands the tray to me.

Sitting up, I take it from her. I don't say anything. There's no point. I start to eat my toast and drink my tea and they realise I'm not going to say anything to them so they get up and leave. As Mother closes the door, she says, "Half an hour until Felicity comes to do your hair. Go have a shower when you've finished breakfast and try to look happy." She slams the door shut behind her. The tears start to flow.

I thought I had cried too many tears when I went to see Scottie. He listened to me moaning about Jonathan and he let me cry on his shoulder then we got drunk and he put me in a taxi to bring me home.

After finishing my breakfast, I shower and start getting ready for my 'special' day. I drag myself around the room like a moody teenager. I don't know how I'm going to paste a smile on my face thinking about what is going to happen tonight when everyone leaves and he takes me to the honeymoon suite. I shudder even thinking about it.

My door opens and Felicity comes in and gives me a hug. "Jennifer, darling. This is so exciting. I can't believe you're getting married. Now, show me this dress and let me see what I can do to your hair to make you stunning."

I smile at her, unzip the dress cover, and pull the base of the dress out of the bag so she can see it. She gasps. When I turn around, she has a big smile on her face and she's trying hard to hide her laugh.

"Are you really getting married in that?" she asks incredulously.

"Yes, I am. Don't you like it?"

"How did you get your father to agree to that?"

"I persuaded Mother and she persuaded him. I don't want to know what she had to do to get him to agree."

She laughs. "I absolutely love it. You are going to be making a statement. 'Fuck tradition' and after everything they have put you through the last six months, then go for it."

I hug her. She understands. "Come on then. Let's see what you have planned with my hair."

She makes me sit on a chair in front of the mirror and she dries it to give it volume. "Are you game for something different?" she asks almost in a whisper.

My eyes sparkle. "Hell yeah! This is going to be a circus anyway, so let's give them even more to talk about."

"Oh, it's definitely going to be a circus. Did you see the amount of photographers camping outside? I hope your father has had the foresight to think of security to get you to the church unscathed."

I don't even want to know, and I certainly don't want to look out the window and give them something to snap. "Just make me beautiful!" I say, looking in the mirror.

"You already are, Jennifer. You just don't believe it yourself." She picks up her bag, puts it on the dressing table, and starts rifling through it. I watch, intrigued, wondering what she is going to bring out.

"Here they are!" She holds something up in the air.

I scrunch my eyes to try and see what she's holding and, slowly, understanding comes.

"Oh my God. Felicity, is that pink hair?" I turn to face her and reach out to touch the pink strings she has in her hands.

"Yes, it sure is. I didn't realise you had a bright pink dress to go with it. I just thought you might like a bit of Pinkie there with you to help you get through the day."

"I can't believe you did that for me. Thank you so much." Tears flow; I can't believe how kind she is being.

"Stop crying. I need your eyes bright and white, not pink or red."

I laugh and wipe up my tears. She sets to work curling, pining, adding in pink, standing back and looking, using more clips, all while I just sit there watching her masterpiece come to life.

When she's happy, she stands back and asks, "Well, what do you think?"

I look in the mirror and I can't believe what I'm seeing.

"I love it. It's sophisticated, elegant, and so sexy.

Thank you so much, Felicity." She has given me volume at the front and underneath some of the layers is the pink hair, then she has used pin curls at the back and nape of my neck to give the impression that I have long hair pinned up. As I look at the back, I can see all the little curls, and when I look at it from the side, I can see the pieces of hair fall like a waterfall into the curls at the back. Every now and again, I see a streak of pink. It's perfect.

She claps her hands together really fast and it reminds me of Beau when he was trying to get out attention.

"Right, now I'm going to do your make-up too."

She gets her make-up out and starts to work on my face. Halfway through, my mother comes into the room. She is dressed in a really stuffy dress and jacket. It's something my grandmother, God rest her soul, would have worn to a funeral. Good to see she's made an effort.

"Your hair is gorgeous," she says. I wasn't expecting that. "Felicity, you have done a marvellous job."

"Thank you."

Another ten minutes and Felicity has finished the make-up. It is very subtle but there is a hint of pink on my eyes and I silently say thank you to her. I look beautiful. I wonder what Nate would think. I bet he wouldn't let me out of the room until he showed me what he thought. I smile, thinking about what he would do to me. Then I remember I'm not marrying him. I'm marrying Jonathan.

I think Felicity sees something cross my face and she says, "Come on. I'll help you into your dress." She reaches out to take it out of the bag and then she lays it down on the bed. She pulls it out onto the floor and opens is so I can step into it; it's the only way to get into it.

I hold her shoulder and step in. Then she pulls it up over my hips, then up further on my body. With each inch she covers, I can feel myself getting suffocated. It feels like she is slowly tying a noose around my neck and all I'm waiting for is the last part before I'm fully hanged.

She pulls the zip up and smooths out the dress and then slowly turns me around to face the floor length mirror on my wall.

"Oh, you are so beautiful," my mother says.

I open my eyes and look at my reflection. I can't believe it's me.

Felicity reaches into the bottom of my wardrobe and brings out my shoes. They are covered in diamantes from the toe to the heel; they are real princess shoes.

"Wow, can I borrow these sometime? They are so exquisite."

I laugh. "You can have them after today."

She lifts the bottom of the dress up so she can reach in and slip them on my feet. Then I stand tall and she adjusts my dress. Perfect!

"Come on. Your father is waiting for you downstairs," Mother says. "We have to do a detour so the press don't know where we're going. We want to try and get rid of this media circus outside. We will have to cover you in a white sheet so they can't see the dress, otherwise it will be all over the internet before we know it."

We all walk out of the room and they go ahead of me down the stairs. Father is waiting for me at the bottom, and he turns to look at me. I slowly descend the stairs, staring straight ahead of me. He smiles and holds out his hand for me. When I reach the bottom, I take it.

"You look beautiful, Jennifer. I wasn't sure about the dress, but you can carry it off." He kisses my hand and then slips my arm through the crook of his. "Your carriage awaits."

As we get to the front door, my mother puts a white sheet over me. "You're going to have to trust your father to get you to the car."

I don't like it one bit, but as soon as we're outside I hear the shouting and cat calling.

"Jennifer, this way..."

"Pinkie, let's see what you're wearing..."

"Why are you going through with this?"

"What about true love? Doesn't it always win?"

"Are you Jennifer or Pinkie today?"

And on it goes.

Safely in the car, I still can't take the sheet off as they are camped along the road. Some of them are in their cars and following us as we peel away from the gate.

"Here, Miss," I hear someone say from the front of the car. "It's going to be warm under there. Have this drink. It will cool you down." He reaches under the sheet and hands me a bottle of water. I take a sip; lovely and cold.

"Father, do I really have to go through with this? Would you really disown me if I didn't marry Jonathan?" I sigh. This is the first time I have really spoken to him about all of this.

"Jennifer, I know you look beautiful and you think a bit of romance will soften me, but yes, I would disown you. This is the right thing for you to do. You made the right choice."

"For who? Not for me, that's for sure. You didn't hear what that man was saying to me. I don't like being in a room on my own with him and you're forcing me to marry him."

"Jonathan is a very well-respected man. He will be

good to you and you will appreciate him. He's not ugly. I hear he's quite good-looking."

"It's not about that, Father. It doesn't matter anyway. I made my decision, but I lost so much along the way."

"Stop talking nonsense. You are getting married to Jonathan and that is that." I feel him move away from me to his side of the car.

I try to compose myself. In the next half an hour, we will be at the church and I will be getting married to a man I don't love.

I hear the driver tell father that he has lost the media and that we will be at the church in ten minutes.

I take deep breaths, trying to calm my already frayed nerves. The car slows down.

I hear a security guy outside the car door. "She's on the premises. Opening the door in three... two... one." The car door opens and he helps me out. He takes my arm and moves me to the church as quickly as he can. He says, "We're walking through the front door and we've closed the door behind us."

When I hear the thud of the big church doors behind me, someone takes the white sheet off me. Felicity is next to me. I don't even know how she got here, but she has her comb, some pins, and some hairspray to touch my hair up so that it doesn't look flattened by the sheet.

She leans into me and whispers, "You look beautiful. You can still change your mind, you know?"

I gasp. Wow, did she just say that I could walk back out of here and walk away from this life? I think she did.

"Thanks, Felicity," I say hugging her. "I have to do this for my parents, for me, and for my friends. I can't have my father ruin their lives like he is ruining mine. This is the easiest option. Believe me when I tell you that I have thought of many different scenarios and this one is the best all round."

"It was worth a try." She smiles at me. "I'm going to go through now, so when you're ready, I'll let the organ player know."

I nod. My father comes to stand at the side of me. All of a sudden, I feel sick. "Father, I need to go to the bathroom. I don't feel well." I'm hot and sweaty and I start to feel clammy.

He rolls his eyes to heaven. "For God's sake, Jennifer. Can't you wait until after the ceremony?"

I shake my head and put my hand over my mouth. He moans and then opens the double doors into the church. I see him trying to gesticulate to someone. Felicity sees him and comes rushing to the back. Before the doors close, I catch a glimpse of Whiskey, Sawyer, Beau, and Scottie. Oh my God. They came to my wedding.

The doors close, but not before Whiskey looks at me and smiles. Then she winks at me. I want to burst into tears but I really think I'm going to vomit.

"Felicity, she needs to find the bathroom. Can you take her, please, and don't take too long. We can't keep the vicar waiting."

Felicity takes my arm and brings me through the vestry to the bathroom. We open the door and I stand over the toilet, bending at the waist.

"Why do I feel so sick, Felicity? I was fine earlier."

"It must be your nerves," she says, looking around her. "You'll be fine in a few minutes, I promise. I'll get you a sip of water. That should make you feel a little bit better." She smiles and then goes back into the vestry to get me a glass of water.

I take a sip and then she hands me a tissue to dab my mouth, otherwise I will end up with lipstick all over my face. After a few minutes, I feel a little bit better and we leave the bathroom.

"Felicity, did you see my friends from Whiskey Sour are here? I can't believe they came."

"They obviously care about you a lot," she says, smiling.

"Yes, they must."

"Especially Nate." She holds both of my hands in front of me.

Gasping, I say, "Is he here? Don't tell me he came

to watch me marry Jonathan? I won't be able to do it if I know he's here watching." I can feel my heart speeding up. I'm getting clammy again. I hope I don't vomit all over this beautiful dress.

"He's not going to watch you marry Jonathan. He couldn't do that. He cares about you too much."

"How do you know that? How do you know him?" I try to back away from her. She's scaring me.

"I know him really well. You see, he's my brother."

"Brother? I never knew you had a brother!"

I feel someone walk into the room behind me. My skin prickles with anticipation. The hairs on my arms and the rest of my body stand on end.

I stare at Felicity. "I... I don't want to turn around. I don't want to be disappointed when he's not there."

I close my eyes and try to smell the air around me.

"Duchess." A deep voice booms, resonating through my body and landing in my core.

I gasp. "Nate?"

"Duchess, did you really believe I would let you go so easily?" He steps closer to me. I feel him touch my waist and all my tensions slide away. He slowly turns me to face him, and smiling back at me is my handsome, beautiful man who I love more than anything.

"Nate." I don't know what to say. I'm so bewildered about him being here.

He leans forward and slowly kisses me on the lips. "My beautiful, gorgeous love of my life."

I turn to look at Felicity, but she's gone. I didn't hear the door open or close. All I could hear was Nate.

I look him up and down, taking in every inch of him. He has on a black tuxedo with a white dress shirt. His bow tie is bright pink. I smile as I reach out to touch it.

He flinches. "Don't touch it. It took Whiskey ages to make it and she will kill me if it comes undone." He chuckles. I still reach out and touch it before I look at his face. He has his beard neatly shaven so that it's tight to his face. His man bun is tied at the back of his head with a pink bobbin.

"There seems to be a theme with your outfit," I say, smiling as he pulls me closer to him. "God, I've missed you." I look up at him and take in his beauty.

"Not as much as I've missed you."

"Jennifer, I don't care if you are vomiting rings around yourself! You need to get out here now! The vicar isn't going to wait much longer," my father shouts from outside the door.

I look at Nate. "I... I have to go!" I look down to the floor. I don't want to leave and he has just made it so much harder for me.

"Duchess." He puts his finger under my chin and moves it so that I have to look up to him. "Duchess, you're not going to marry that fuckwit today. You are going to marry me instead."

"What? Are you joking?" I say, trying to pull away from him.

"Duchess, I love you. I need you. I know you love me and need me too. I wanted to ask you to marry me before all this drama kicked off but I didn't want to scare you away. I want to spend the rest of my life with you. I want to have children with you. I want to grow old with you and I want to love you forever. Will you marry me?" he says as he goes down on one knee and holds out a jewellery box which contains the most beautiful platinum ring with a pink diamond.

"I can't."

"Why? Because of Jonathan the fifty-third or whoever he is?" he asks, nodding towards the door.

"You know why. My parents will ruin Whiskey Sour. They will ruin you. I don't care about myself. This is all for you so that you can get on with your lives without me." A lone tear leaves my eye and rolls down my face.

He gets up from the floor and takes my hands in his. "Do you love me?"

I nod.

"Do you want to spend the rest of your life with me?"

I nod.

"That's all I need to hear." He reaches down and lifts me up bridal style and starts to walk out the back door, where he obviously came in.

"Nate, what about the wedding? What about the people in there?"

"Those people weren't there to see you get married, they were there to gossip about you and what everyone is wearing, and they think they are going to become celebrities overnight."

We're walking down the path at the side of the church to a limo, which I hadn't seen earlier. As we approach the limo, the door is flung open.

"These are the people who want to see you get married because they love you. These people right here." He slides us both into the limo, and already seated inside are Whiskey, Sawyer, Scottie, Beau, and Felicity.

"Oh my God. Guys, did you just kidnap me from my wedding?" I laugh as someone hands me a glass of champagne.

"We sure did," Whiskey says, clinking my glass. "Back where you belong with people who love you."

I can feel the tears freefalling now. I don't even bother to wipe them away.

Nate has his arm around me and has me pulled in tight. He keeps leaning down and kissing me on the head.

"What's going to happen now? Are you guys sure you want to do this? My parents will come after you all, not just Nate and me. That's why I was going through with it, because of all of you."

"Don't worry about what's going to happen with your parents. You've missed out on a lot since you've been gone. Everything will work out. First, though, we have a wedding to go to," Nate says.

"What? But we just left my wedding. Who's getting married?"

"We are!" he says matter-of-factly. "You know you want to. You know I will wear you down and get you to agree to this. You know you really want to wear my beautiful pink ring. Most of all, you know you want to spend the rest of your life with me, because I feel the same way."

My mouth drops open. I really don't know what to say. I look around at everyone else who is nodding at me as if they're trying to make me say yes.

"Yes. Yes, of course I want to be with you for the rest of your life. You've got a lot of explaining to do though."

"I know, but I won't be doing it until after we're married, after we've celebrated with our friends, and after I've been buried deep inside you... at least five times."

Everyone in the limo groans. "Nate, did you have to give us that visual?" his sister asks.

"I kind of like that visual," I say, laughing. I can't believe she is his sister. I need to have words with both of them about this news.

"So where are we going?" I ask.

"Somewhere special," Nate says mysteriously. "I am going to blindfold you as it's a surprise."

He reaches into his pocket and takes out his pink pocket square and unfolds it slowly while I watch him intently. I see it's a blindfold and he gently puts it on me.

I'm trying to work out where we're going by the direction of the limo, but I don't do a good job. I haven't got a clue.

When the limo pulls up, Nate gets out first and then takes my hands to help me up. I feel someone smoothing down my dress and guess it's Felicity. Nate then takes my arm and puts it through the crook of his and guides me into a building.

I can hear it has a big wooden door and the smell is kind of familiar. We go through another door and there is a big cheer. "Nate, I want to take my blindfold off please."

He chuckles. "You're not one for surprises, are you?" I can feel he is undoing the blindfold, and when my eyes get used to the light, I see all my Whiskey Sour friends, Scottie's friends, Drew, and some of our very regular and trustworthy customers.

"We... we can't get married here! It won't be legal." He smiles at me and takes a piece of paper out of his pocket.

I take it with shaky hands. As I read it, I see that Whiskey Sour has been pre-approved and licensed for marriage ceremonies.

"When? How?" I stutter.

"You can thank Scottie for that one," Nate says. "Ages ago, I spoke to Scottie and asked him if he thought you would marry me. He said yes. I mean, why would you turn me down?" he says, turning this way and that. I laugh. "I approached Whiskey about seeing if we could hold a wedding here and when she said yes, we arranged it. Then came your bombshell, but I still wasn't going to let you go easily. When you left, I was beside myself. My plans had all failed but I had to let you go. That was the hardest part. Letting you believe that I was letting you go forever. We had to wait for Drew to come up with a plan to make this happen." I turn to face Drew and smile at him.

"What if I didn't leave the church today?"

He laughs. "There was no chance I was leaving that church without you, duchess. There was no other outcome." He pulls me close and kisses me. "Now, can we stop talking and get married?"

I nod. "This conversation isn't over though," I warn him.

"Can it at least wait until after I've fucked you?" he says with wide eyes.

I feel hot all over and I know that he is the one I will spend the rest of my days with.

"Come on then. Let's do this so we can party!" I say, laughing.

Everyone gets into place and the registrar nods his head to start the music.

Nate walks down the aisle beside me. Nothing is traditional with him. Nothing is traditional with this wedding. Nothing is traditional with us. That's what makes us special though. That's what makes us happy.

Everything we have been through has brought us to this moment.

"I do!"

THE END

ALMOST

Nate

Three Years Later

"Duchess, come on. We're going to be late. What the fuck are you doing?" She is taking her time. We need to hurry up.

"Coming. Stop being grouchy," she shouts from upstairs. She comes out of our room and starts to walk down the stairs and I catch my breath. She is so gorgeous and I love her so much. She looks different now than when I first met her, but she is more beautiful every day. Gone is the pink hair. She now has bright, hot pink streaks in her hair like she did on our wedding day, but they are permanent now. Gone are the beige clothes and all the bright pink and black ones. She has finally found her own style and she is one hot woman.

Holding her hand is a little girl who is just learning to walk down the stairs. She looks at me and smiles. "Dada. Dada." There is no sweeter sound than your daughter calling you, unless of course you count my wife when she comes and screams my name.

I hold out my arms for Bella to come to me and she slowly makes her way down the stairs, holding her mum's hand. When she reaches the second from bottom step, she launches herself in the air, knowing I'll catch her. I'll always catch her.

I swing her around and she giggles. That sound is enough to make me start laughing. I hold my hand out to Pinkie to help her down the last few steps as she's finding it harder and harder each day with her blossoming stomach. We found out today that she's having a boy. I'm so happy. I can't believe I'm going to be a father again, and to a baby boy. I kiss her when she finally makes it to the bottom step.

"Just wait 'til I get you on our own tonight," I threaten.

"I can't wait," she says with hunger in her eyes.

We are going to see Gracie, Snow's daughter, in her first ballet. She is a beautiful child, just like her mother, and she adores Spence. We have all grown extremely close, closer than we were before we had our women. It's our family and it's all we need.

Things have changed a lot for us since we got

married. I spent the next day telling her what had happened, how Felicity and I had not been allowed to see each other for the last eight years because I didn't follow in my father's footsteps and go into the family business. She was at home, much like Jennifer, and she was waiting to meet someone who was suitable for her to be married off to. We kept in touch and met up regularly, but it was only when everything came out in the press that she realised that she knew Jennifer from 'the circuit' and that they were friends.

We talked about how I felt about her and she was on board with the plan from the start. It definitely brought Felicity and me back together.

I then had to explain to her how I had gone to her parents, offering them money to pay them back what they would lose from her not marrying Jonathan. She was appalled when they turned me down, even when they knew how much I loved her. It was obviously about more than the money at that stage. However, after she married me, her family didn't have a leg to stand on. We paid back the money she had used during those six months, and after that, she never went home again. They couldn't sue her or me, because we paid off our debts.

Now we live in a large house in Holland Park with more money than we know what to do with. We still work at Whiskey Sour. Not every night, but always together. Felicity comes over to watch Bella. She loves her and loves spending that time with her.

Our Whiskey Sour journey has been full of ups and downs, but in those dark times, there was always someone looking for us.

Whiskey Sour is our family.

Thank you for reading PINKIE as part of the standalone Whiskey Sour Series. I really hope you enjoyed it and that you'll consider leaving a review on Amazon. It's a great way to help other readers discover new books. Click here to leave a review.

If you like PINKIE and would like to read more, turn the page for a list of my other books. And if you don't want to miss any future releases, please join my http://eepurl.com/djEztr

BETSEY – Book 4 in the Whiskey Sour standalone series.

Betsey is a living, breathing, fifties chick. She loves the movies, the songs, the clothes and the lifestyle. She's a nurse who looks after anyone that she can. Her

Grampy is sick, and she does what she can to help him and make him comfortable.

Billie is gorgeous, funny and extremely sexy. Wearing slick clothes, leather jackets, telling jokes and singing songs, Billie is the newest member of the Whiskey Sour team.

After a traumatic experience Betsey doesn't want any man to touch her but, somehow, she's attracted to Billie and doesn't understand it.

Follow their story of forbidden love, rejection and heartbreak for the ones that they love.

Warning: There are extremely tasteful and sensual scenes of F/F which are vital to the story, if this offends you then please do not read.

Acknowledgements

Once again thank you to all my readers for taking time out of their busy lives to read one of my books. It seriously amazes me how everyone loves my words. I try to put a small piece of me into each of the books that I write. However, there are a couple that stand out because they have a lot of me in them. PINKIE is one of them. I used my humour and sarcasm to fine tune Pinkie into the sassy woman that she has become. I love WHISKEY and didn't think that I would feel the same way about another character in this series, but Pinkie gives me all the feels. I love her.

Thank you to my editor Kyra Lennon for fine tuning my book to make it better to read. You always do such great work with my books and I am so thankful to have you beside me.

My PA, Natasha, you are always there for me and talk

me down on the ledge so many times, thank you. Jen, you are never too far away and you help me so much with my social media that I need to thank you for helping to make me more visible so that people can see my books in the first place.

JC, your formatting is the bomb!

Jade from SteamPower thank you so much for this gorgeous cover. I love all the Whiskey Sour covers, they are individual and custom drawn. I can't wait to see what you do with the next one!

Finally a thank you to my friend, Karen. You know who you are and you're are there when I need to run ideas past you and you usually message me when I need it the most. It's like you feel my emotions and for that I am grateful.

Thank you to Christine from The Next Step PR for organising the cover reveal and release day blitz for me. Your work is outstanding.

Hope you have enjoyed Pinkie and I look forward to bringing you BETSEY later this year.

EROTIC ROMANCE

The Lust Train – Newsletter Exclusive Standalone

MIXOLOGY Series

Hunter

Keaton

Zac

DARK ROMANCE

My One Regret - Standalone

WHISKEY SOUR Series

Whiskey

Snow

TILL DEATH US DO PART Series

Till Death Us Do Part – Trilogy (For Better or For Worse, In Sickness and In Health, To Love and To Cherish)

To Have or To Hold – Standalone in Till Death Us Do Part Series

For Richer or For Poorer – Standalone in Till Death Us Do Part Series

CHOCOLATE BOX ROMANCE

Beauty Within

o-Love in 6 Minutes

A Taste of Christmas Dublin Style

ROMANTIC COMEDY

Eff This Diet – Standalone

SUSHINE TOUR Series

Sunshine in Madrid

Sunshine at Christmas